THE NORTH CHINA LOVER

Other works by Marguerite Duras

Marguerite Duras

The
North China
Lover

Translated by Leigh Hafrey

THE NEW PRESS / NEW YORK

Published in the United States by The New Press, New York.
Distributed by W. W. Norton, New York.

Library of Congress Cataloging in Publication Data

Duras, Marguerite.
[Amant de la Chine du Nord.   English]
The North China lover / Marguerite Duras. — 1st ed.
p.   cm.
ISBN 1-56584-018-6
I. Title
PQ2607.U8245A62613   1992
843'.912—dc20
92-53729 CIP

BOOK DESIGN BY GINA DAVIS

Printed in the United States of America

FOR THANH

This book could have been called *Love in the Street,* or *The Lover's Story,* or *The Lover Revisited.* In the end, I had a choice of two broader, truer titles: *The North China Lover* or *North China.*

I learned that he had been dead for some years. That was May 1990, a year ago now. I had never thought of him dead. Also, they told me he was buried at Sadec; the blue house was still there, with his family and some children living in it. People in Sadec had loved him for his kindness, his simplicity; also, he had become very religious toward the end of his life.

I stopped the work I was doing. I wrote the story of the North China lover and the child: it wasn't quite there in *The Lover,* I hadn't given them enough time. Writing this book made me deliriously happy. The novel kept me a year, enclosed me in that year of the love between the Chinese man and the child.

I didn't go beyond the ocean liner's departure, which is to say, the child's departure.

I could never have imagined the Chinese dying, his body dying, his skin, his sex, his hands. For a whole year I went back to the days when I would cross the Mekong River, on the ferry to Vinh-Long.

In the blinding light of the retelling, Thanh's face suddenly appeared—and the little brother's, the child who was different.

The story enclosed me with these people, and with them only.

I became a novelist all over again.

Marguerite Duras
May 1991

A house in the middle of a schoolyard. Everything is wide open. Like a party. There are Strauss and Franz Lehar waltzes, but also "Ramona" and "China Nights" coming out the windows and doors. Water is running everywhere, inside and out.

They're washing down the house. It gets a bath like this two or three times a year. Houseboy friends and neighborhood children have come to watch. They help out with pailsful of water, they wash the floor tiles, the walls, the tables. They dance to the European music as they wash. They're laughing. They're singing.

It's a party, lively, happy.

The music, that's the mother, a French lady playing the piano in the next room.

Among the dancers is a very young man, French, handsome, he dances with a very young girl, also French. They look alike.

She is the one who has no name in the first book, or the one before it, or in this one.

He is Paulo, the little brother the young sister worships, the one who isn't named.

Another young man joins the party: that's Pierre. The older brother.

He positions himself a few yards from the party and watches.

He watches the party for a long time.

And then, he does it: he pushes the little houseboys out of the way; they scatter in fright. He moves forward. He reaches the couple, the little brother and the sister.

And then, he does it: he grabs the little brother by the shoulders, he shoves him over to the open upstairs window. And as though driven to it by some cruel need, he throws him out like a dog.

The young brother picks himself up and takes off without looking back, screaming wordlessly.

The young sister follows him: she jumps through the window and catches up with him. He is lying stretched out against the hedge by the yard, crying, trembling, he says he'd sooner die than—than what? He no longer knows, he's already forgotten, he hasn't said it was the big brother.

The mother had returned to the piano. But the neighborhood children didn't come back. And then the houseboys fled the house that the children had deserted.

Night has fallen. The setting is the same.

4

The mother is still there, where the "party" was that afternoon.

Everything is back in order. The furniture is in place.

The mother doesn't expect a thing. She is at the center of her kingdom—this family we've glimpsed here.

The mother never interferes anymore. She will never interfere again.

She will let things happen as they must.

All through the story told here.

She is a disheartened mother.

The older brother is watching the mother. He smiles at her. The mother doesn't see him.

This is a book.
This is a film.
This is night.

The voice speaking is the written voice of the book.
A blind voice. Faceless.
Very young.
Silent.

This is a straight road. Lit by gas lamps.
Cobblestoned, it seems. Ancient.
Lined with giant trees.
Ancient.

There are white, terraced villas on either side of the street. Surrounded by fences and grounds.

This is an outpost in southern French Indochina.
The year is 1930.
This is the French quarter.
This is a street in the French quarter.
The night smells of jasmine.
Mingling with the dull, sweet smell of the river.

Someone is walking ahead of us. It isn't the speaker.
She's a very young girl, or possibly a child. She looks like one. She has a supple stride. She is barefoot. Slim. Maybe even skinny. Her legs, yes, absolutely—a child. Come of age.
She walks toward the river.

The yellow light from the hurricane lamps, the joy, the calls, the laughter at the bottom of the street—yes, this is the river. The Mekong.
This is a floating village.
This is where the delta begins. Where the river ends.

That's dance music we're hearing by the road, from the grounds alongside. It comes from the gardens of the General

Administration building. A record. Probably forgotten, playing across the deserted grounds.

The Post party must have been here, behind the fence surrounding the grounds. It's a recording of an American dance tune that has been popular for some months now.

The girl angles off toward the grounds, she goes to have a look at where the party was, behind the fence. We follow her. We stop, facing the grounds.

In the glow of a streetlamp, a white path crosses the grounds. It is empty.
And then a woman in a long, dark-red dress moves slowly down the white space of the path. She comes from the river. She disappears into the residence.

The party must have ended early because of the heat. All that's left is a forgotten record playing in the desert.

The woman in red hasn't reappeared. She must be inside the residence.

The terraces on the second floor have gone dark, and shortly after her passing, lights on the ground floor have gone on, at the heart of the residence.

The path stays empty.
The woman in red doesn't come back.

The girl goes back to the street. She vanishes among the trees. And then, here she is again. She is still walking toward the river.

She is in front of us. It is still hard to make out her face in the yellow light from the street. But it seems that, yes, she is very young. A child perhaps. A white child.

The path, too, has gone dark. The woman in red hasn't come back.
What remains is that weak light at the heart of the residence.

Shortly after the path goes dark, there's that tune coming

from the residence, a dead waltz played on the piano. Out of a story. No telling which one anymore.

The girl stops. She listens. We can see her listening.
She has turned her head toward the music and has closed her eyes. Her blind gaze is fixed.
We can see her better. Very young—yes, she is. Still a child. She cries.
The girl is still. The girl is crying.

In the film, we won't give the waltz a name.
Here in the book, we will call it: "The Desperation Waltz."

The girl will be listening to it even after it ends.

In the film, here in this book, we will call her the Child.

The child leaves the picture. She walks off-camera and away from the party.

The camera slowly scans what we've just seen, then turns and starts off again in the direction the child has taken.

The street is empty again. The Mekong has vanished.
It is lighter now.

There is nothing more to see except the vanished Mekong
and the straight, dark street.

This is a gate.
This is a schoolyard.
It's the same night. The same child.
This is a school. The yard is of beaten earth.
It is bare and gleaming, smoothed by the bare feet of the
children on the post.

This is a French school. They'd written it on the gate:
French School for Girls in the City of Vinh-Long.

The child opens the gate.
Closes it again.

Crosses the empty yard.
Goes into the schoolmistress's house.

We lose sight of her.
We stay in the empty yard.

In the emptiness left by the child, a third melody begins, interrupted by wild, strident laughter, screams. That's the Ganges beggarwoman, crossing the post as she does every night. Always trying to get to the sea, the Chittagong road, the dead children's road, the Asian beggars who have tried for a thousand years to reach the fish-swarming waters of the Sound.

This is the mother and child's bedroom.

It is a colonial bedroom. Poorly lit. No night tables. A single bulb on the ceiling. It is furnished with a big iron double bed and a wardrobe with a mirror. The bed is colonial, with a black varnish, decorated with brass balls at the four corners of the canopy, also black. It looks like a cage. The bed is draped to the floor in a vast, snowy-white mosquito netting. No pillows, just hard horsehair bolsters. No top sheet. The feet on the bed sit in containers of water and pounded glass, isolating them from that curse of the colonies, the creatures of the tropical night.

The mother is in bed.

She isn't sleeping.

She is waiting for her child.

Here she is. She comes in from outside. She crosses the

room. Perhaps we recognize her silhouette, her dress. Yes, she's the one who was walking toward the river along the straight road past the grounds.

She goes toward the shower. We hear the sound of water. She comes back.

That's when we see her. Yes. She is definitely still a child. Still skinny, still almost flat-chested. She has long, curly auburn hair, she is wearing native clogs made of a light wood with leather straps. She has bright green eyes flecked with brown. Her dead father's eyes, they say. Yes, she was the child crying over the waltz on the straight road. She was also the one who knew that the woman playing that waltz was the woman dressed in red who had walked down the white path. And who knew that she, the child, was the only one in the whole post who knew those things. The whole post and beyond. That's what kind of child she was. She is wearing the same white cotton chemise as her mother, made by Dô, with straps added.

She parts the two flaps of the mosquito netting, quickly tucks it under the mattress, at the same time slips through the opening in the netting, closes it again. The mother wasn't asleep. She sits up beside the child and braids her hair for the night. She does it mechanically, without looking.

In the distance, faintly, the murmur of the village on the river, which only subsides at dawn.

The child asks:

"Have you seen Paulo?"

"He came in, he ate in the kitchen with Thanh. Then he went out again."

The child says she went to the party to see if he was there, but the party was over, everyone had gone.

She also says she will go find him later, she knows where he must be hiding. She doesn't worry when he is outside, far from the house. She knows he always waits for her when he has run away, so he doesn't have to come home by himself, in case Pierre is waiting there to hit him again. The mother says it's when he is outside that she's afraid—of snakes, of madmen, and also that he might take off, just like that, that all of a sudden he might not recognize anything, and run away. She says that can happen with children like that.

The child, it's Pierre she's afraid of. He might kill Paulo. Might kill him without even knowing it, she says.

She also says:

"What you're telling me isn't true. You aren't afraid for Paulo. You're only afraid for Pierre."

The mother doesn't register what her daughter is saying. Suddenly tender, she gives her a long look, beyond their immediate conversation. And changes the subject as she does so:

"What will you write about when you write your books?"

The child cries:

"Paulo. You. And Pierre too, but just so I can kill him off."

She turns abruptly toward her mother, she nestles up against her in tears. And then she cries out again very softly:

"Why is it you love him that way but not us, not ever . . ."

The mother lies:

"I love my three children all the same."

The child goes on complaining. It makes you want to shut her up. To slap her.

15

"It's not true, it's not true. You're a liar. Answer me this once. Why do you love him like that and not us?"

Silence. And the mother breathes an answer:

"I don't know why."

A long pause. She adds:

"I've never known . . ."

Crying, the child lies down on her mother's body and kisses her. Puts a hand over her mouth to stop her from talking anymore about her love.

The mother lets herself be insulted, abused. She is still off in that other part of her life where blind preference takes her. Sealed off. Lost. Beyond all anger.

The child pleads with her, but it does no good.

"If he doesn't leave the house, he'll kill Paulo someday. And you know it. That's what's so awful . . ."

Tonelessly, under her breath, the mother says she knows it. And, as it happens, the previous evening she had written Saigon to ask that her son be repatriated to France.

The child sits up. She gives a low cry of relief and pain.

"Did you really?"

"Yes."

"For sure?"

The mother explains.

"This time, for sure. He robbed the opium den again the day before yesterday. I paid them again, one last time. And then I wrote to the Bureau for Repatriation. And this time I mailed the letter the same night."

The child hugs the mother. The mother doesn't cry—a corpse.

The child cries softly:

"It's so awful to have it come to that . . . it's so awful."

The mother says yes, it probably is, but she can't tell anymore, not her . . . yes, it must really be awful, but she, she really can't tell at all anymore. The mother and child hug each other. The mother still without a single tear. Killed by life.

The child asks whether he knows he's leaving.

The mother says no, that that was the hardest part—having to tell him it was over.

The mother strokes her daughter's hair. She says:

"Don't pity him. It's awful for a mother to have to say this, but I'll say it just the same: he isn't worth it. You have to realize that: it isn't worth suffering for someone like Pierre."

Silence from the child. The mother adds:

"What I mean is, Pierre isn't worth saving anymore. Because it's all over for Pierre, it's too late, he's ruined."

The child cries through her tears:

"That's why you love him."

"I don't really know—probably. Yes, that's part of it, and that's why you're crying, too. It comes to the same thing."

The mother takes the child in her arms. And she says to her:

"But I also love you very much, you and Paulo."

The child pulled away from her mother then and looked at her. She saw her mother had been speaking in all innocence. The child was set to scream at her, curse her, kill her. She only smiled at her.

The mother went on talking to her "little girl," her last child, telling her she had lied about the reasons for repatriating Pierre, for sending him away. That it wasn't only because of the opium.

17

The mother explains:*

"One or two months ago, I'm not sure now, I was in Dô's room when you came in for dinner, you and Paulo. I didn't give myself away. I do that sometimes, only you don't know it—I hide in Dô's room so I can see all three of you together. Thanh appeared as he usually does, he put the thit-kho and the rice on the table, and he went out.

"So Paulo took a helping. Then Pierre came in. Paulo had taken the biggest piece from the dish of thit-kho and you had let him. But when Pierre showed up, you got scared. Pierre didn't sit down right away. He looked at his empty plate, and he looked at Paulo's plate. He laughed. He had a fixed smile, frightening. I told myself that was how he would smile when he was dead. At first Paulo laughed, he said:

"'I was just joking.'

"Pierre took the piece of meat off Paulo's plate and put it on his own. And he ate it—the way a dog would. And he howled just like a dog, that's really what he was.

"'Listen, stupid. You know the biggest pieces are for me.'

"It was you who protested. You asked:

"'Why are they for you?'

"And he said:

"'Because that's how it is.'

"And you protested violently. I was afraid people would hear you in the street. You yelled:

"'I wish you were dead.'

---

*For a movie, we can choose. We can stay with the face of the mother as she talks. Or we can see the table and children as the mother *talks about them*. The author prefers the latter option.

18

"Pierre had his fists clenched, ready to beat in Paulo's face. Paulo started crying. Pierre yelled:

"'Out! Get out of here, right now!'

"You ran off, you and Paulo."

The child apologizes for yelling at her mother. They cry together, stretched out straight in bed.

The mother says:

"That's when I began to understand that I couldn't be trusted. That Paulo was in mortal danger because of me. And I only wrote Saigon yesterday to have him repatriated. Pierre . . . for me, it's as if he were even more mortal than the rest."

Silence. The mother turns to her daughter, crying this time.

"Without you, Paulo would have been dead a long time ago. And I knew it. That's the worst part: I knew it."

A long silence.

The child is seized with rage. She shouts:

"You never knew. I love Paulo more than anything in the world. More than you. More than anything. He's been living in fear of you and Pierre for a long time, Paulo. He's like my fiancé, Paulo, my child, he's my greatest treasure . . ."

"I know it."

The child shouts:

"No you don't. You don't know anything."

The child calms down. She takes her mother in her arms. She speaks to her with a sudden softness, she tells her:

"You don't know anything anymore. You have to realize that. Not a thing. You think you know and you don't know anything. You only know about him, about Pierre. You don't know anything about Paulo and me anymore. It's not your fault. That's just how it is. Nothing at all. Don't worry about it."

Silence.

The mother's face is set, frightened.

The child's face is just as horrified. They face each other stiffly. And suddenly they lower their eyes in shame.

It's the mother who lowers her eyes. And is still. As though she's been killed. And then remembers the child outside and cries:

"Go find Paulo. Go on, quickly now—suddenly I'm afraid for him."

The mother adds:

"You're going back to school tomorrow, you ought to get in the habit of going to bed earlier, you're already a night person like me."

"It's all the same . . ."

"No it isn't."

The child is in the entryway to the house, over by the dining room that looks onto the large schoolyard. Everything is open.

We see her from behind, facing the terrace and the street.

She's searching for her little brother. She looks. Goes in among the trees. Looks under the bushes.

Suddenly, it's as though she dissolves in the moonlight, then reappears.

We see her in different parts of the yard. She is barefoot, silent, wearing a child's nightshirt.

She vanishes into an empty classroom.

Reappears in the big moonlit yard.

And then we see her looking at something she sees but we cannot yet: Paulo. We see her going toward him, the little brother from the dance. He is sleeping in the arcade that runs the length of the classrooms, behind a low wall, shaded from the moonlight. She stops. She lies down beside him. She looks at him as though he were sacred.

He is sound asleep. His eyes half-open, like "those" children's. He has the smooth, untouched face of those "other" children.

She kisses his hair, his face, his hands folded on his chest. She calls, she calls him very softly: Paulo.

He is sleeping.

She gets up and calls him even more softly: Paulo. My treasure. My little child.

He wakes. He looks at her. And then he recognizes her. She says:

"Come to bed."

He gets up. He follows her.

The night birds are singing.

The little brother stops. He listens to the birds. He goes on. She says to him:

"Don't be afraid anymore. Not of anyone. Not Pierre. Not anything. Nothing. Ever again. Listen to me: not ever again. Swear it."

The little brother swears it. And then he forgets. He says:

"The moon is waking up the birds."

They walk away. The yard is empty again. We lose them. They reappear. They walk on through the schoolyards. They don't speak.

And then the child stops and points at the sky. She says: "Look at the sky, Paulo."

Paulo stops and looks at the sky. He repeats the words: *the sky . . . the birds . . .*

We can see the sky, see it from one edge of the earth to the other, it's a blue lacquer sparkling with light.

We see the two children looking at the sky together. And then we see them looking at it separately.

And then we see Thanh coming in from the street and going toward the two children.

Then we see the blue sky bursting with light again.

Then we hear Thanh whistling that wordless waltz, the "Desperation Waltz," against a still of the blue sky.

When they were very little, in the dry season their mother sometimes took them to see the night. She told them to look hard at that sky, as blue as in full day, that lighting of the earth as far as the eye could see. And to listen hard to the sounds in the night, the people calling, laughing, singing, and the howling of dogs haunted by death; and you had to listen to them, too, all those calls that spoke of the hell of solitude, as well as the beauty of the songs that spoke of that solitude. Children really ought to be told the things people usually hid from them— work, wars, parting, injustice, solitude, death. Yes, the hellish but inescapable side of life, children needed to be told that, too—it was like looking at the sky, the beauty of the world's nights. The mother's children had often asked her to explain what she meant by that. The mother had always answered her children by saying she didn't know, that no one knew. And that you had to know that, too. Know above all else: that you knew nothing. That even when mothers told their children they knew everything, they didn't.

The mother. She also reminded them, her children, that this land of Indochina was their true homeland. This was where they had been born, and where she had met their father, the only man she had ever loved. The man they hadn't known, because they were too young when he died and still so young after his death that she had spoken of it very little in order not to darken their childhood. And time had also passed, and her love for her children had taken over her life. And then the mother cried. And then, in an unknown language, Thanh sang the story of his life on the border of Siam when the mother had found him and brought him back to the bungalow with her other children. To teach him French, she said, and to stay clean and eat well, day in and day out.

The child remembered, too, she cried with Thanh when he sang that song he called the "Song of Childhood Long Ago," which told everything we've just said, to the tune of the "Desperation Waltz."

This is the river.

This is the ferry across the Mekong. The ferry in the books. On the river.

There on the ferry is the native bus, the long black Léon Bollée cars, the North China lovers, looking.

The ferry sets out.

Once it departs, the child gets off the bus. She looks at the river. She also looks at the elegant Chinese who is inside the big black car.

She is made up, the child, dressed like the young girl in the books: the dress made of yellowed white native silk; the man's hat, all "childhood and innocence"—supple felt, flat-brimmed, rosewood-colored, with a wide black band; and those very worn, completely down-at-the-heel party shoes—black lamé, if you please—patterned with rhinestones.

The man who gets out of the black limousine is other than the one in the book, but still Manchurian. He is a little different from the one in the book: he's a little more solid than the other, less frightened than the other, bolder. He is better-looking, more robust. He is more "cinematic" than the one in the book. And he's also less timid facing the child.

She, she has stayed the way she was in the book, small, skinny, tough, hard to get a sense of, hard to label, less pretty than she looks, poor, the daughter of poor people, poor ancestors, farmers, cobblers, always first in French at all her schools, yet disgusted by France, and mourning the country of her birth and youth, spitting out the red meat of Western steaks, with a taste for weak men, and sexy like you've never seen before. Wild about reading, seeing—fresh, free.

Him, he's Chinese. A tall Chinese. He has the white skin of the North Chinese. He is very elegant. He has on the raw silk suit and mahogany-colored English shoes young Saigon bankers wear.

He looks at her.

They look at each other. Smile at each other. He comes over.

He's smoking a 555. She is very young. There is a little fear in his hand, which trembles—just barely—as he offers her a cigarette.

"Do you smoke?"

The child gestures no.

26

"Excuse me. It's such a surprise to find someone like you here. You can't imagine . . ."

The child doesn't answer. She doesn't smile. She gives him a straight look. A look you could call unabashed. Fresh. Not right, her mother calls it: "You don't look at people that way." It's almost as if she weren't hearing what he says. She looks at the clothes, the car. There is the scent of a European cologne about him, and the fainter one of opium and silk, tussore silk, amber silk, amber skin. She takes it all in. The chauffeur, the car, and then him again, the Chinese. Her childishness surfaces in the misplaced curiosity of her glance, always startling, insatiable. He looks at her looking at all the novelties the ferry carries that day.

This is where his own curiosity begins.

The child says:

"What kind of car is that?"

"A Morris Léon Bollée."

The child mimes her ignorance. She laughs.

She says:

"Never even heard the name . . ."

He laughs along with her. She asks:

"Who are you?

"I live in Sadec."

"Where in Sadec?"

"By the river, it's the big house with terraces. Just outside Sadec."

The child searches her memory and sees which one. She says:

"The light blue, China blue house—"

"That's right. Light China blue."

He smiles. She looks at him. He says:

"I've never seen you in Sadec."

"My mother was posted to Sadec two years ago, and I'm at boarding school in Saigon. That's why."

Silence. The Chinese says:

"You missed Vinh-Long . . ."

"Yes. It's what we've liked best."

They smile at each other.

She asks.

"And you?"

"Me—I'm back from Paris. I studied in France for three years. I've been back a few months."

"What were you studying?"

"Nothing much, it's nothing worth mentioning. And you?"

I'm doing my baccalaureate at Chasseloup-Laubat Secondary School. I board at Lyautey School."

As though it mattered somehow, she adds:

"I was born in Indochina. My brothers, too. We were all born here."

She looks at the river. He is intrigued. His fear has left him. He smiles. He talks. He says:

"I can give you a lift to Saigon if you like."

She doesn't hesitate. The car, and him with his mocking look—she is pleased. You can tell by the smile in her eyes. She'll tell her little brother Paulo about the Léon Bollée. That, he'll understand.

"All right."

The Chinese tells his chauffeur—in Chinese—to take the

child's suitcase off the bus and put it in the Léon Bollée. Which the chauffeur does.

The cars have driven up the ramp, off the ferry. They're on the bank. The people follow on foot. They gather round the roadside stands. The child looks at the cakes, made of corn soaked in coconut milk, sweetened with molasses and wrapped in a banana leaf.

The Chinese treats her to one. She takes it. She devours it. She doesn't say thank you.

Where is she from?

Her slenderness suggests a half-caste, but no, her eyes are too light.

He watches her devouring the cake. That's when he starts using the familiar *tu*.

"Do you want another?"

She sees he's laughing. No, she says, she doesn't.

The second ferry has left the other shore. It is coming nearer.

Suddenly the child is fascinated by the sight of the approaching ferry. The child forgets the Chinese.

On the other ferry, she has just recognized the black Lancia convertible of the woman in the red dress from the waltz the other night.

The Chinese asks who it is.

The child is slow to answer. She doesn't answer the Chinese. She says the names "just to say them." In a sort of secret incantation, she says:

"It's Mme. Stretter. Anne-Marie Stretter. The General Administrator's wife. In Vinh-Long, they call her A.M.S. . . ."

She smiles, apologizes for knowing so much about her.

The Chinese is intrigued by what the child is saying. He says he must have heard people talk about that woman in Sadec. But he says he doesn't know anything about her. And then, suddenly, he does remember it after all, that name . . .

The child says:

"She has a lot of lovers, that's what you're remembering . . ."

"Yes, I guess so. That must be it . . ."

"There was one very young one, he supposedly killed himself over her. I don't know the whole story."

"She is beautiful. I thought she'd be younger—people say she's a little crazy, right?"

The child can't say if she's crazy. She says:

"I don't know about crazy."

The car—they're off again. They're on the road to Saigon. He gives her a straight look. The Chinese will intersperse his still involuntary use of the familiar *tu* with the formal *vous*:

"People often give you rides on the ferry, don't they."

She gestures yes.

"Sometimes you say no?"

She gestures yes, sometimes.

"Like when there are very small kids who cry all the time . . ."

They both laugh, a little too much. They seem distracted. They have the same laugh. Their own way of laughing.

After they've laughed, she looks outside. Then he, he takes in the marks of her poverty. The scuffed black satin shoes, the "native" suitcase made of pasteboard, the man's hat. He laughs. His laugh makes her laugh.

"You go to school wearing those shoes?"

The girl looks at her shoes. It's almost as though she were seeing them for the first time. And she laughs with him. She says yes . . .

"And that hat, too?"

Yes. That too. She laughs even harder. She's in hysterics, her laugh is so spontaneous. He laughs with her, the same way.

"Still, it really suits you—it's amazing how well that hat suits you, as though it had been made for you . . ."

She asks, laughing:

"What about the shoes?"

The Chinese laughs even harder. He says:

"I don't know about the shoes."

They're in hysterics looking at the black shoes.

This is where, this was where the story turned itself around, after their fit of hysterical giggling.

31

They stop laughing. They look away. Outside, rice paddies as far as the eye can see. Empty sky. Pale heat. Veiled sun.

And little roads all around for the ox carts the children guide.

They are shut in together, in the twilight of the car.

It's this stopping of motion, of speech, this pretense of watching the monotony outside, the road, the light, the rice paddies to the edge of the sky, that little by little silences the story.

The Chinese no longer talks to the child. It's as though he were neglecting her. As though he were caught up in the trip. He looks out. She, she looks at his hand on the armrest of the back seat. He has forgotten that hand. Time passes. And then, without fully realizing what she's doing, she takes it. She looks at it. She holds it like an object she's never seen that close up before: a Chinese hand, a Chinese man's hand. It's thin, it crooks toward the nails, it might almost be broken, charmingly crippled, it has the grace of a dead bird's wing.

There's a signet ring on the fourth finger, with a diamond set in the middle, where the gold is thickest.

It is too big, that ring, too heavy for the fourth finger of that hand. That hand—she can't really say, but it must be beautiful, it is darker than the rest of the arm. The child doesn't look at the watch by the hand. Nor the ring. She is fascinated with the hand. She touches it, "just to see." The hand is sleeping. It doesn't move.

And then, slowly, she leans over the hand.

She inhales it. She looks at it.

Looks at the naked hand.

Then suddenly stops. Doesn't look at it anymore.

She doesn't know if he is sleeping or not. She lets go of the hand. No, it seems he isn't sleeping. She can't tell. She turns the hand over, very gingerly, she looks at the other side of that hand, the naked inside, she touches the silky skin, coated with a cool dampness. Then she puts the thing back where it was on the armrest. She puts it away. The hand docilely submits.

We see nothing from the Chinese, nothing, not a sign of his waking up. Maybe he's asleep.

The child turns away, toward the outside, the rice paddies, the Chinese. The air trembles with heat.

It's a little as though she had carried the hand into sleep with her and kept it.

She leaves the hand far away from her. She doesn't look at it.

She falls asleep.

She seems to have fallen asleep.

She knows it isn't so; she does—she believes it isn't so. We can't tell.

Was the Chinese asleep? She will never know. She never found out. When she woke up, he was looking at her. He had seen her falling asleep and that was when she had woken up.

They don't talk about the hand. As though nothing had ever happened. He says:

"What grade are you in?"

"Eleventh grade."

"How old are you?"

A very slight hesitation on the child's part.

"Sixteen."

The Chinese doubts it.

"You're very small for sixteen."

"I've always been small, I'll be small the rest of my life."

He gives her a very straight look. She doesn't look at him. He asks:

"You lie sometimes . . ."

"No."

"How can that be? How do you keep from lying?"

"I don't talk."

He laughs. She says:

"Also, lying scares me. I can't stop myself, it's a little like dying."

She adds, she asserts:

"You don't lie, do you."

He looks at her. He thinks it over. Astonished, he says:

"You're right. How strange . . ."

"You didn't realize it?"

"No. I had forgotten, or maybe . . . I never knew."

She looks at him. She believes him. She says:

"How do you keep from lying?"

"I don't. It's probably because I don't have anything in my life to deny. I don't know."

She wants to kiss him. He sees that, he smiles at her. She says:

"You would have told your mother."

"What about?"

She hesitates, she says:

"About what has happened to us."

They look at each other. He's about to say he doesn't understand. He says:

"Yes. First thing. We would have talked the whole night. She loved things like that—surprises, I suppose people call them?"

"Yes. You could also call them something else."

He looks at her. He says:

"And you. Your mother . . . will you tell her?"

"Just," she laughs, "just thinking about it—"

The Chinese grins at the child. He says:

"Nothing at all? Ever?"

"Nothing. Ever. Nothing."

She takes his hand, kisses the hand.

He looks at her with his eyes closed.

She says:

"You're wrong, you wouldn't have told your mother anything."

She smiles gently, sweetly. She looks at him.

He says:

"Aside from that, I'm twenty-seven years old. Unemployed . . ."

"And Chinese on top of it—"

"On top of it, yes." He looks at her closely. "You really are delightful. Have people told you that before?"

She smiles.

"No."

"And beautiful? Haven't you been told that you're beautiful?"

No, she hasn't been told that. That she is small, yes, but not beautiful. She says:

"No," and smiles, "not yet."

He looks at her. He says:

"You like hearing that . . ."

"Yes."

The Chinese laughs in a different way. She laughs with him.

"So no one's ever said anything to you . . ."

"Nothing."

"And that they wanted you—have they told you that? They have told you that—how could they not have?"

The child laughs, but not the same way.

"Oh yes, kids—but it didn't mean anything, they were teasing me. Mostly half-castes. Never any French."

The Chinese doesn't laugh. He asks:

"What about Chinese?"

The child smiles. She says, astonished:

"Never any Chinese, either, that's true . . ."

Silence.

The Chinese suddenly smiles like a child.

"And you, do you like going to school?"

She thinks it over, she says she doesn't really know whether she likes it or not, but maybe—yes, maybe she does. He says that, for himself, he would have liked to study humanities at the university in Peking. That his mother agreed. That it was his father who hadn't wanted it. For Chinese of their generation, it was French and American English you had to learn. He

36

was forgetting—he also spent a year in America for just that reason.

"So you could be what, afterwards . . ."

"A banker," he grins, "like all the men in my family for the last hundred years."

She says the blue house is the most beautiful one in Vinh-Long and Sadec put together, he must be a millionaire, his father.

He laughs, he says in China children never know how much their father is worth.

He was forgetting: every year he goes for training in the big Peking banks. He tells her that.

She says:

"Not in Manchuria?"

No. In Peking. He says, for his father, Manchuria isn't wealthy enough, given what the family fortune is currently worth.

They pass through villages of rice, children, and dogs. The children play on the road between the rows of huts. They're protected by the dogs, those yellow, skinny ones from the country. When the car has gone by, you can see the parents peering over the embankments to see if they're all still there, the children and the dogs.

It's after the village that she falls asleep again. When you have a chauffeur to drive you, you always fall asleep on the roads of Camau, between the rice paddies and the sky.

She opens her eyes. She closes them again. They stop talking. She lets him do as he pleases. He says:

37

"Close your eyes."

She closes her eyes, the way he wants.

His hand strokes the child's face, her lips, her closed eyes. Her sleep is perfect—he knows she isn't sleeping, he prefers it that way.

In a low voice, very slowly, he says a long sentence in Chinese.

With her eyes closed, she asks him what he said. He says that on her body, hers—that he can't say what it is, this is the first time this is happening to him . . .

The hand stops suddenly. She opens her eyes and closes them again. The hand starts again. The hand is soft, it is never sudden, it has a steady discreetness, an age-old gentility, of the skin, of the soul.

He closed his eyes, too, when he stroked her eyes, her lips. The hand leaves her face, descends the length of her body. Sometimes it stops, frightened. Then it withdraws.

He looks at her.

He turns away, toward the outside.

With the same gentleness as his hand shows, he asks how old she really is.

She hesitates. She says apologetically:

"I'm still small."

"How many years?"

She answers the way a Chinese would:

"Sixteen years."

"No," he smiles, "that isn't true."

"Fifteen years, fifteen and a half—all right?"

He laughs.

"All right."

38

Silence.

"What is it you want?"

The child doesn't answer. Maybe she doesn't understand.

The Chinese doesn't put it as a question, he says:

"You've never made love."

The child doesn't answer. She tries to answer. She doesn't know how to answer that. He is drawn toward her. From her silence he can tell there's something she wants to say. Something she doesn't know how to say yet and that she only knows, probably, by its being forbidden. He says:

"Forgive me . . ."

They look outside.

They look at the sea of rice paddies of Cochin China. The watery plain crisscrossed by little, straight white roads for the children's carts. The unmoving, monumental hell of the heat. As far as the eye can see, the fabulous, silken flatness of the delta. Later she will speak, the child, of a vague country, from her childhood, a tropical Flanders barely rescued from the sea.

They cross the expanse without speaking.

And then it is she who does the talking: the southern lands of South Indochina were on the same level as the sea for millions of years before there was life on earth, and the peasants still do what the first men did, taking ground from the sea and enclosing it behind hard earthen dikes and leaving it there for years and years to wash out the salt with rain water and make a rice paddy imprisoned by man for all time. She says:

"I was born here, in the South, and my brothers, too. So our mother tells us about the country."

The child is dozing. When she wakes up, the Chinese tells her A.M.S. has passed them. She was driving, the chauffeur was next to her. The child says she often does the driving. She hesitates, and says:

"She sleeps with her chauffeurs just like she does with the princes when they visit Cochin China—the Laotians, Cambodians."

"And you believe that."

She hesitates again, and then she tells him:

"Yes. Once she slept with my little brother. She saw him at the Club one evening, she invited him to play tennis. He went. Afterwards they went to the pool on the grounds. There's a bungalow there with showers, workout rooms, it's almost always deserted."

The Chinese says:

"Maybe your little brother is a king, too."

The child smiles. She doesn't answer. It strikes her it's true, her little brother really is a prince. A prisoner in his difference from others, alone in the palace of his solitude, so far away, so alone that living for him is almost like being born again each day.

The Chinese looks at her:

"You're crying."

"It's what you said about Paulo. It's so true . . ."

He asks again, very low.

"Was he the one who told you?"

"No. Him, he doesn't say a thing, almost nothing—but I know everything he'd say if he talked."

She remembers, laughs through her tears:

"After that, he didn't want to go to the tennis courts with A.M.S., didn't want to play with her. He was scared . . ."

"Of what?"

"I don't know." Then it dawns on her: "It's true—you can never tell what my little brother's scared of. You never know before it happens."

"What is it you like so much about that woman . . ."

She thinks about it. She's never asked herself that question. She says:

"The story, I guess."

They enter a different phase of the trip. The villages are more numerous, the roads better. The car has slowed down.

He says:

"We're almost in Cholon. You like Saigon, or Cholon?"

She smiles:

"All I know are the posts out in the bush. What about you?"

"Me? Yes, I like Cholon. I like China. And Cholon is China. But New York and San Francisco, no."

They fall silent. He spoke with his chauffeur again. He tells the child the chauffeur knows Lyautey Boarding School.

They look out at the approaching city.

They were about to separate. She remembers how difficult, how cruel it was to speak. They couldn't find words, their desire was so strong. They hadn't looked at each other again. They had avoided each other's hands, eyes. It was he who had imposed the silence. She would say later that you could have told they were in love by that silence alone, the words the silence skirted,

41

its very pace, how it diverted them, and the game, too, the childishness of that game and the tears.

They drive on for quite a while longer. Without talking. The child knows he won't say another word. He knows that about her, the same way.

The story is already there, already unavoidable,
A story of blinding love,
Always about to be,
Never forgotten.

The black car has come to a stop in front of Lyautey Boarding School. The chauffeur takes the child's suitcase and carries it to the door of the school.

The child gets out of the car, she goes slowly, docilely, toward the same door.

The Chinese doesn't watch her.

They don't look around, don't look at each other again. Don't know each other anymore.

This is the courtyard at Lyautey Boarding School.

The light is less bright. It is evening. The treetops are already in twilight. The courtyard is weakly lit by a network of green-and-white metal lamps. The girls' games are supervised.

There are about fifty girls there. Some are on outdoor benches, on the steps of the connecting passageways, some are walking the length of the buildings in pairs, chatting and laughing excitedly over anything and everything.

There's one stretched out on a bench, the one called here and in the other books by her real name, the one who is so wondrously beautiful yet claims she is ugly, the one with that heavenly name, Hélène Lagonelle, from Dalat. The child's other, never-to-be-forgotten, love.

She looks at her and then slowly strokes her face.

Hélène Lagonelle wakes up. They smile at each other.

Hélène Lagonelle says that later on she will tell her about something awful that has happened at Lyautey Boarding School. She says:

"That's why I was waiting for you, and then I fell asleep. You're back earlier than usual."

"I met someone on the ferry who was all by himself and offered me a ride in his car."

"A white?"

"No. A Chinese."

"Sometimes they're handsome, the Chinese."

"Especially the ones from the north. Which he was."

They look at each other. The child particularly.

"You didn't go to Dalat?"

"No. My parents couldn't come get me. They didn't say why. But I wasn't bored."

The child looks at her attentively, suddenly uneasy about the black shadows under Hélène's eyes and her pale face. She asks her:

"You don't think you might be sick?"

"No, but I'm always tired. They gave me a tonic in the infirmary."

"What did they tell you?"

"That it was nothing. Maybe laziness, or my still getting used to the climate—after Dalat."

The child tries to overcome a kind of uneasiness, but she can't, she never will quite. The uneasiness will persist until they're separated.*

"Didn't you have something to tell me?"

Then, in a rush, Hélène Lagonelle tells her what has happened at Lyautey Boarding School.

"Would you believe it, the monitors discovered one of the girls is prostituting herself out back every night. We hadn't noticed a thing. You know her—it's Alice, the half-caste . . ."

Silence.

"Alice—who does she do it with?"

"Anyone. Passers-by. Men in cars who stop—she goes with them, too. They go into the ditch behind the dormitory; always at the same spot."

Silence.

"You've seen them—"

Hélène Lagonelle lies:

"No, The others, they told me it wasn't worth looking, you can't see a thing."

---

*Hélène Lagonelle died of tuberculosis at Pau, in France, to which her family returned ten years after she left Lyautey Boarding School. She was twenty-seven years old. She had come back from Indochina, where she had gotten married. She had two children. She was still just as beautiful. This from aunts of hers who called after the publication of *The Lover*.

The child asks what Alice says about prostituting herself.

"She says she likes it—a lot, even; that you don't know the men, you don't see them, or almost don't, and that's what makes her have a—how do you say it . . ."

The child hesitates, and then she says the word, "for Alice."

She says: orgasm.

Hélène says, that's it.

They look at each other and laugh, happy to see each other again.

Hélène says:

"My mother says you shouldn't say that word, even when you understand it. That it's a bad word. What word does your little brother say?"

"He doesn't. My little brother doesn't say anything. He doesn't know anything. He knows it exists. You'll see, the first time it happens to us—you're afraid, you think you're going to die. But he must think the word is hidden, my little brother. That there is no special word for things you can't see."

"Talk to me some more about your little brother."

"The same story all over again?"

"Yes. It's never the same, but you, you don't know that."

"We'd go hunting together in the forest by the mouth of the channel. Always by ourselves. And then one time it happened. He got into bed with me. Brothers and sisters, we're strangers to each other. We were still very little, maybe seven, eight years old, he got into bed and then he came back every night. One time my older brother saw him. He beat him up. That's when it started, the fear he might kill him. And after that, my mother made me sleep in her bed. But we went on doing it anyway. When we were at Prey-Nop, evenings, we

45

went into the forest, or on boats. At Sadec, we'd go into an empty classroom."

"And then?"

"Then he turned ten, then twelve, and then thirteen. And once he came. He forgot everything then, he was so happy he cried. I cried, too. It was like a celebration—but deep, you know, it made you cry, not laugh."

The child cries. Hélène Lagonelle cries with her. They always cried together without knowing why, out of feeling, love, childhood, exile.

Hélène says:

"I knew you were nuts, but never this bad."

"Why am I nuts?"

"I can't explain it, but you are nuts, believe me. Maybe it's because of your little brother, you love him so much it drives you crazy . . ."

Silence. And then Hélène Lagonelle asks the question:

"Before me, had you told anyone all about your little brother?"

"Thanh, once. It was at night, in the car, we were on our way to Prey-Nop."

"He cried, Thanh."

"I don't know, I fell asleep."

The child stops, and then she goes on:

"And anyway, I'm sure Paulo will find other women some-day, in Vinh-Long, Saigon, even white women, at the movies, on the street, and of course, especially on the Sadec ferry."

They laugh.

Hélène asks the child about Thanh, whether or not they've ever made love.

46

The child says:

"He never wanted to. I asked him a lot of times, but he never wanted to."

Hélène starts crying. She says:

"You're going to leave for France and I'll be all alone. I don't think my parents want me in Dalat anymore. They don't love me anymore."

Silence. And then Hélène forgets her destiny. She starts talking about Alice again, the one who makes love in the ditches. She speaks in a low voice. She says:

"I haven't told you everything. Alice takes money, a lot of it. She's doing it so she can buy a house. Alice is an orphan, she has no relatives, nothing. She says if she has a house, even a little one, at least she'll always have that to go to. She says you never know."

The child always believes what Hélène says. She says:

"I believe what you're saying, but maybe it's not just because of the house that she makes the men pay and they come back. Maybe they like it that way too—how much does she charge?"

"Ten piastres. And time after time, the same night."

"Ten piastres isn't bad, is it?"

"It sounds all right to me. But I don't know anything about their rates. Alice does, though—even for the white women down on rue Catinat."

The child. She has tears in her eyes. Hélène Lagonelle takes her in her arms, she cries:

"What's wrong? Is it what I said?"

The child smiles at Hélène. She says it's nothing, it's when people talk about money, and because of some of the stuff in her own life.

They kiss, and they stay kissing, hugging each other, kissing, being still, loving each other very hard.

And then Hélène starts talking to the child again. She says:

"There's something else I wanted to tell you—it's that I'm like Alice. She likes that life. And I'd like it, too. I know I would. And I have to say, I'd prefer being a prostitute to taking care of lepers . . ."

The child laughs:

"What's this now . . ."

"Well, everyone here knows it except you. What do you think's going on? They're supposed to be making us study so we can find work when we get out of boarding school, but it's not true. They take us in and then send us off to clinics for lepers, plague and cholera victims. Otherwise they couldn't get anyone to do it . . ."

The child laughs hard:

"And I suppose you really believe that story?"

"Cross my heart and hope to die."

"You always believe the worst, don't you."

"Always."

They laugh. Still, Hélène Lagonelle doesn't question Alice's story.

The child asks Hélène Lagonelle what else Alice has been saying about the matter.

Hélène says Alice finds it perfectly natural. She says no two men are alike, just as it is everywhere and with everything. There are some very very special ones, too. And there are also some who are afraid to do it. But what Alice likes best, and there are a lot of these, are the men who talk to her as if she were just another woman, who call her by all sorts of names, who even speak to her in other languages. Or they talk about their wives—there are a lot of those, too. And there are some who insult her. And there are others who say she's the only one they've ever loved.

The two friends laugh. The child asks:

"Is Alice afraid sometimes?"

"What does she have to be afraid of?"

"A murderer, a maniac. You don't know, what if . . ."

"She didn't say, but maybe a little, just the same. You never know in this part of town, do you?"

"No. But it's the whites who say that, and they never come around here, so . . ."

Hélène Lagonelle gives the child a long look, and then she asks:

"Are you afraid of the Chinese?"

"I guess a little, but maybe more of loving him. I'm afraid—I want to love only Paulo till the day I die."

"I knew it was that, something like that . . ."

Hélène cries. The child takes her in her arms and talks to her the way a lover would.

And Hélène is happy and she says the child is crazy to be saying those things to her. She doesn't say which things . . .

The child no longer knows what she's saying to Hélène. And Hélène is suddenly seized by the fear, the one awful fear among all others, that she is deceiving herself about the true nature of this passion they have for one another, making them more and more alone together wherever they go.

This is the road to school. The time is seven-thirty, it's morning. In Saigon. There's the wonderful freshness of the streets after the municipal water carts have passed, the time when the smell of jasmine inundates the city—so powerful some whites "find it appalling" when they first arrive. And then miss it once they've left the colony.

The child is coming from Lyautey Boarding School. She is on her way to her school.

At this hour, rue Lyautey is practically deserted.

The child is the only one from the boarding school who goes to the lycée in Saigon, and so she's the only one to pass this way.

This is the beginning of the story.

The child doesn't know it yet.

50

And then, suddenly, the story is there, stopped ahead of her along the other sidewalk to her left, the car from the ferry, very long and very black, so gorgeous, gorgeous, and expensive, too, so big. Like a room in a Grand Hotel.

The child doesn't recognize it at first. She stands there, stopped in front of it. Looking at it. And then recognizing it. And then recognizing him. And then seeing him, him, the man from Manchuria, asleep, or dead. The one with the hand, the one from the trip.

He acts as though he hasn't seen her.
He is where he was, to the right on the back seat.
She sees him without having to look at him.

The chauffeur is also in his place, just right, his head also turned away from the child, who is slowly—you might almost say absentmindedly—crossing the street.

For her, the child, their "meeting by chance" in this part of town had always remained what began their story, what had made them the lovers in the books she had written.

She thought, she knew that it was there, out there, from somewhere beyond all reason, from a kind of awareness they had had of their desire, that they had no longer denied them-selves anything, that they had become lovers.

Maybe she wonders whether she should, or maybe she doesn't know she has already crossed the expanse of street that separates them.

51

At the very first, she doesn't move.

She goes slowly toward him behind the window.

Stays there.

They look at each other very quickly, just enough to see, to have seen each other.

The car's direction is opposite to her own line of travel. She puts her hand on the window. Then she takes away her hand and puts her mouth on the glass, kisses there, lets her mouth settle there. Her eyes are closed like in the movies.

It's as though they had made love in the street, she said.

That strong.

The Chinese had looked.

Then he had lowered his eyes.

Dead from wanting this child.

Martyred.

The child had recrossed the street.

Without turning back, she went on toward school.

She heard the car depart without making any noise on a road suddenly turned velvet, nocturnal.

In the months that followed, they never once talked about the frightful pain of their need for each other.

School.

There are no students in the hallways now. They have all gone into their classrooms.

The child is late.

She goes into her classroom. She says, "Excuse me."

The teacher is discussing Louise Labé.

He and the child smile at each other.

The teacher goes on with his discussion of Louise Labé—he refuses to call her by her epithet, "*la belle Cordière.*" First he gives his personal opinion of Louise Labé. He says he has tremendous admiration for her, that she is one of the few people from a bygone era he would have liked to meet and hear recite their poetry.

The teacher tells how, when Louise Labé went to her printer-bookseller to deliver the manuscript of her latest collection, she always asked a woman friend to come along. She had remained vague when she had to explain why she wanted that, a woman companion, for the one who had written the poems. The teacher said the company might have served as authentification, especially coming from a woman. The teacher said it was up to the students to see in it what they thought. A boy said Louise Labé was afraid of men trying to pick her up on the roads. A girl said she was afraid of having her poems stolen. The child said that the two women, Louise Labé and the one who kept her company, probably knew each other so well that Louise Labé never asked herself whether she took her along because of the poems, or for some other reason.

This is Thursday afternoon. Almost all the boarders are going for a walk.

They cross the central courtyard. They line up in pairs. All in the white dress of the school uniform, the white canvas shoes, the white belts and the hats, also white canvas. Washable.

The boarding school empties out. As soon as the boarders have gone, an abyss of silence develops in the central courtyard, brought on, it would seem, by the total and sudden absence of voices.

This is a sheltered spot in the empty boarding school. It's at the point where two hallways meet, and a door leads to the classrooms connected with the boarding facility. From that sheltered spot, you can hear the voices of the two girlfriends, and a dance tune. It comes from a record player set on the ground. The tune is a standard paso doble, the one for the kill in the arenas of Spain. It is a brutal tune, with a magnificently vulgar beat.

They talk little, except for the child's pointers on the dance step.

They are barefoot on the flagstones in the hall. They are wearing the short dresses in fashion then, light-colored cottons with equally light flowered prints.

They are pretty, they have forgotten they already know that.

They dance. They are white. They need only ask to be exempted from the walk that is required of the abandoned half-castes, because, no matter how poor their families, they are white.

Hélène Lagonelle asks the child who taught her the paso doble.

"My little brother, Paulo."

"He's taught you everything, your little brother."

"Yes."

The silence is total when the voices cease.

Hélène Lagonelle says she is falling in love with Paulo.

She says she doesn't understand why her parents leave her there. She isn't studying, not at all. She says her parents know it, they're trying to get rid of her. Why, she doesn't know.

"I can't stand the thought of being here another three years. I'd rather die."

The child laughs:

"Since when can't you stand it?"

"Since you met the Chinese."

Silence. The child bursts out laughing:

"So it's been three days now?"

"Yes, but it began a while ago, very strong. And that isn't all. I've been lying to you, too. I've started thinking about your little brother, at night . . ."

They're in the cool shade. They dance. There's sunlight coming through a high window, like in a prison, or a convent, so the men can't come in. Disturbing in their own right, their unbuckled sandals lie where they've been thrown, in a corner in the sun.

A young houseboy in white is sitting against one of the columns in the hallway, one of the ones who sings the Indochinese songs from the girls' childhood at night over by the kitchens. He watches them. He doesn't move, as though nailed in place by his gaze on them, the white girls who dance for him alone and don't know it.

Hélène Lagonelle speaks under her breath to the child: "Are you going to sleep with the Chinese?"

"Yes, I think so."

"When?"

"Maybe later on today."

"Do you want him very much?"

"Very much."

"Do you have a date?"

"No, but it doesn't matter."

"You're sure he'll come?"

"Yes."

"What is it you like about him?"

"I don't know. Why are you crying, did you like things better before?"

"Yes and no. Since the holidays I've begun thinking about your little brother, and loving him. His skin, his hands—and you'd been saying how you dreamed about him. Sometimes at night I'd call out to him. And then, once . . . I just wanted to tell you."

The child finishes Hélène's phrase:

"Once it happened to you."

"Yes. I lied to you. I tell you lies and you don't even know it. You don't care . . ."

Silence. The child says:

"I can tell there's something else you want to say."

Hélène gives the child a squeeze, hides her face in her hands and says:

"I'd like to do it once with the men who do it with Alice. Just once. I wanted to talk to you about it . . ."

The child cries in a low voice:

"No. They've all got syphilis."

"Can it kill you?"

"Yes. I know my older brother had it. A French doctor saved him."

"So what am I going to do?"

"You'll wait for France. Or else you'll go home to Dalat without warning. And stay there. Not go anywhere."

Silence.

"I want all the houseboys. And that guy on the record. The teachers. The Chinese."

"It's true. It takes over your whole body. It's all you think about."

Silence.

They look at each other.

The child has tears in her eyes. She says:

"I want to tell you something. I can't say it, but I want you to know. For me, the first time I wanted someone was you. The first day. After you got here. It was in the morning, you were coming back from the showers, stark naked. I couldn't believe my eyes, I thought I was imagining you . . ."

The child pulls away from Hélène Lagonelle and they look at each other.

Hélène says:

"I knew that, that story . . ."

"Do you really not know how beautiful you are?"

"Me, I can't tell. Yes, I suppose I may be. My mother, now—she's very beautiful. So it would make sense if I was, too, wouldn't it? But it's as though people said it and meant something else, like I'm not very smart. And I can tell they're being nasty by their look . . ."

The child laughs. She puts her mouth over Hélène's. They kiss. Under her breath, Hélène says:

"You're the one who's beautiful. Why is it I can't even bear to look at myself in the mirror sometimes?"

"Maybe because you're too beautiful. It makes you sick . . ."

The little kitchen boy is still watching the "young French-women" dance; they're kissing again.

The record has ended. The dance is over.

In the deserted boarding school, a silence like sleep.

Then the sound of the car fills the entryway. The girls and the little houseboy go to the window and look. There is the Léon Bollée, stopped at the entrance to the school. You can see the chauffeur of the Léon Bollée. White curtains conceal the rear seats, as though the car were carrying a condemned man one mustn't look at.

The child goes out in her bare feet, her shoes in hand, and she goes over to the car. The chauffeur opens the door for her.

They're sitting side by side.

They don't look at each other. The moment is a hard one. The kind you run away from.

The chauffeur has his orders. He drives off immediately. He steers slowly through the city full of pedestrians, bicycles, the everyday native crowd.

They reach the Cascade. The car stops. The child doesn't

move. She says she doesn't want to go there. The Chinese doesn't ask why. He tells the chauffeur to head back.

The child has pressed herself to the Chinese man. She says in a very low voice:

"I want to go to your place. You know that. Why did you take me to the Cascade?"

He pulls her to him. He says:

"Out of stupidity."

She stays against him, her face hidden in him. She says:

"I'm beginning to want you again. You can't imagine how much I want you . . ."

He tells her she shouldn't say that.

She promises. Never again.

And then he says he wants her, too, the same way.

Back through the Chinese part of the city.

They don't look at the city. When it seems they're looking at it, they're looking at nothing.

They look at each other without wanting to. Then they lower their eyes. Then stay that way, seeing each other through closed eyelids, without moving and without seeing each other, as though they were still looking at each other.

The child says:

"I want you very much."

He says she knows it about herself just as she knows it about him.

They turn away toward the outside.

The Chinese city reaches them in the clamor of old tram-cars, the noise of old wars, old worn-out armies, the tramcars ring their bells constantly as they run. They sound like a ratchet, it makes you want to run away. There are clusters of Cholon children hanging from the trams. There are women with thrilled babies on the roofs, there are wicker baskets full of birds and fruit on the running boards, on the doors' safety chains. The trams have lost their tram shape, they're swollen, lumpy, unrecognizable.

Suddenly the crowd thins out, though it's impossible to say why or how.

There. Now it's peaceful. The noise stays the same, but fades away. The crowd thins out. The women aren't on the run anymore, they're relaxed. This is a street with cubicles like there are all over Indochina. It has the outdoor taps they call fountains. A covered arcade runs the length of it. It has no shops, no trams. Country merchants are resting on the beaten earth in the shadows of the arcade. The racket of Cholon is far away, very far, it's like being in a village in the middle of the city. This is where it is, in this village. It is under this open arcade.

A door.
He opens the door.
It's dark.
It isn't what you'd expect, it is humble. Banal. It is nothing.
He speaks. He says:
"I didn't pick the furniture. It was here, I kept it."
She laughs. She says:
"There isn't any furniture. Look . . ."

60

He looks and he says under his breath she's absolutely right, there is nothing but the bed, the armchair, and the table.

He sits in the armchair. She remains standing.

She looks at him again. She smiles. She says:

"I like it this way . . ."

They don't look at each other. As soon as he closes the door, they both suddenly experience what seems like a lack of interest. Desire doesn't show itself, it vanishes—then, abruptly, it comes back. She looks at him. He doesn't look at her. She's the one who does it. She sees he's afraid.

It's the gentleness in the child's look that helps break the fear. She's the one who wants to know, who wants everything, all of it, everything, life and death at the same time. Who is the closest to the despair and insight that comes with passion—because of the younger brother who grew up in the shadow of the criminal brother and wants to die every day while she, the child, saves him from despair every night.

As though he were required to say it, the Chinese says under his breath:

"I may be falling in love with you."

A sort of fear in the child's eyes. She says nothing.*

Probably to keep busy, she walks slowly, noiselessly around the bachelor quarters, she looks at the place, furnished like a

---

*If this book is made into a film, the child can't just have a pretty face. That could jeopardize the film. There's something else at work in this child—something "hard to get around," an untamed curiosity, a lack of breeding, a lack, yes, of reticence. Some Junior Miss France would bring the whole film down. Worse: it would make it disappear. Beauty doesn't act. It doesn't look. It is looked at.

railway hotel. He doesn't realize it though, he doesn't see those things, and she loves him for it. He watches her at it— investigating the premises—and he doesn't understand why. He thinks she's passing time, dealing with the hell of waiting, that that's the reason. He says:

"It's my father who gave me this place. We call them bachelor quarters. The rich young Chinese here, they have a lot of mistresses, it's the custom."

She repeats the phrase—"bachelor quarters." She says she knows the term, she doesn't know how, maybe from novels. She isn't walking now. She is stopped in front of him, she looks at him, she asks him:

"You have a lot of mistresses."

Her sudden, marvelous use of the familiar *tu* with him.

"Yes, I suppose so, from time to time."

Her gaze goes out to him, very alive, in a flash of happiness—yes, she likes that. He asks:

"You like my having mistresses?"

Yes, she says. She doesn't say why, she can't say.

He is struck by her answer. It frightens him a little. It is a difficult moment for him.

She says she wants the sort of man who loves a woman and the woman doesn't love him. She says the first man she wanted was a man like that, unhappy, shaken by a disappointment in love.

The Chinese asks: Thanh? She says no, not him. He says:

"Listen to me. Let's go. We'll come back some other time . . ."

The child doesn't answer. The Chinese gets up, he takes a couple of steps, he turns his back to her. He says:

62

"You're so young it scares me. I'm afraid I won't be able to
. . . won't be able to cope with the emotion. Can you understand that a little?"

He turns toward her. His smile trembles. She hesitates.
She says she doesn't understand. But she understands a little,
she, too, is a little frightened. He asks:

"You don't know how."

She says she knows a little but she doesn't know if that's
what he means.

Silence.

"How could you know?"

"Through my younger brother—we were very frightened of
our older brother. So we slept in the same bed when we were
little. That's how it started . . ."

Silence.

"You love your little brother."

The child is slow to answer, to talk about the secret in her
life, this little brother who is "different."

"Yes."

"More than anything in the world."

"Yes."

The Chinese is deeply moved:

"He's the one who . . . who's a little different from other
people . . ."

She looks at him. Doesn't answer.

She has tears in her eyes. She still doesn't answer. She asks:

"How do you know that?"

"I don't remember anymore."

Silence. She says:

"It's true, if you live in Sadec you must know about us."

"Before meeting you, no, I didn't. It was after the ferry, the next day. My chauffeur recognized you."

"What did he tell you—say the words."

"He said to me: 'She is the daughter of the head of the girls' school. She has two brothers. They're very poor. The mother was ruined.'"

Suddenly he feels very timid. He can't say why. Maybe it's the child's age that appears suddenly like a blunt, solid, unassailable, almost indecent truth. And her savagery as well, which she no doubt gets from the mother. She, she can't know these things about herself. He asks:

"Is that it?"

"That's it—that's us. How did he put it, about my mother being ruined?"

"He said it was an awful story, that she'd had bad luck."

Silence. She doesn't comment. She doesn't want to comment on that. She asks:

"We can stay here a little longer. It's so hot—outside."

He gets up, turns on the fan. He sits back down. Sees her, looks at her. She, she doesn't take her eyes off him. She asks:

"You don't work."

"No. Not at all."

"You never do anything, ever. You never do anything at all . . ."

"Never."

She smiles at him. She says:

"You say 'never' as though you were saying 'all the time.'"

Her childishness comes back: she takes off her hat. She lets her shoes fall off her feet, she doesn't pick them up.

He looks at her.

Silence.

The Chinese says in a low voice:

"It's strange how attractive I find you . . ."

She goes to stand under the fan. She smiles at the coolness of it. She is pleased. Neither of them notices that love is there. Desire still bides its time.

She goes to another door, opposite the front door. She tries to open it. She turns back to him. You can tell from the way he is looking at her that he is going to fall in love with her, that he isn't mistaken. He's in a kind of constant turmoil, whether she talks or is silent. There's a good deal of play, of childishness, in her exploration of the house. For him, love might have started there. The child fills him with fear and joy. She asks:

"Where's it go, this door?"

He laughs:

"Onto another street. To escape by. What did you think?"

The child smiles at the Chinese. She says:

"A garden. That's not it?"

"No. It's a door for no reason. You'd have preferred . . ."

She comes back, takes a glass from the edge of the sink. She says:

"A door to escape by."

They look at each other. She says:

"I'm thirsty."

"There's filtered water in the icebox by the door."

Silence. Then she says:

"I like the way it is here."

He asks her what way she sees this place as being.

They look at each other. She hesitates, then she says:

"It's neglected"—she gives him a straight look—"and also, it has your smell."

He watches her walking, drinking, coming back.

Forgetting about him, himself. And then remembering. He stands up.

He looks at her. He says:

"I'm going to have you."

Silence. The smile has left the child's face. She has gone pale.

"Come here."

She goes toward him. She says nothing, stops looking at him.

He is sitting in front of her; she is standing. She lowers her eyes. He takes her dress by the hem, lifts it off her. Then he slips off her child's white cotton underpants. He throws the dress and underpants on the chair. He takes his hands off her body, looks at it. Looks at her. She, no. She keeps her eyes lowered, she lets him look.

He gets up. She stays standing before him. She waits. He sits down again. He strokes, but just barely, her still skinny body. Her child's breasts, her stomach. He closes his eyes like a blind man. He stops. He takes away his hands. He opens his eyes. Very low, he says:

"You aren't sixteen years. It isn't true."

No answer from the child. He says: It's a little frightening. He doesn't expect an answer. He laughs and he cries. And she, she watches him and she thinks—with a smile full of tears—that she may be about to love him for the rest of her life.

Almost fearfully, as though she were fragile—but with contained violence, too—he carries her over and puts her on the bed. Once she is there, in place, an offering, he looks at her again and the fear returns. He closes his eyes, he doesn't speak, he doesn't want her anymore. And then she is the one who does it—she. With her eyes closed, she undresses him. One button after another, one sleeve after the other.

He doesn't help her. Doesn't move. Closes his eyes like her.

The child. She's alone in the picture, she looks at the nakedness of his body, as unknown as that of any face, as unique, delightful, as that of his hand on her body during the trip. She looks at him over and over, and he lets her do it, he lets himself be looked at. She says in a low voice:

"They're handsome, Chinese men."

She kisses. She isn't alone in the picture anymore. He is there. Beside her. She kisses with her eyes closed. She takes his hands, puts them to her face. His hands from the trip. She takes them and puts them on her body. And then he moves, he takes her in his arms and he gently rolls onto that skinny, virgin body. And as he slowly covers it with his own body, without touching it yet, the camera might leave the bed; it might veer toward the window, might stop there at the drawn blinds. And then the noise from the street might come in, muffled, distant in the night of the room. And the voice of the Chinese would come as near as his hands.

He says:

"I'm going to hurt you."

67

She says she knows.

He also says that sometimes the woman screams. Chinese women scream. But it only hurts once in a lifetime, and forever.

He says he loves her and doesn't want to lie to her: the pain never comes back, never ever, it's the truth, he swears it.

He tells her that she should close her eyes.

That he's going to do it—going to take her.

That she should close her eyes. My little girl, he says.

She says, no, not with her eyes closed.

She says, all the rest, yes, but not with her eyes closed.

He says, yes, she has to. Because of the blood.

She didn't know about the blood.

She starts to get out of bed.

With his hand, he stops her from getting up.

She doesn't try again.

She would say she remembered the fear. The way she remembered his skin, its softness. And how it, in turn, recoiled.

With her eyes closed, she touched that softness, she touched its golden color, the voice, the frightened heart, the whole of that body suspended above her own, ready to murder her unknowing, she who has become his child. A child of his, the Chinese man, who doesn't speak but cries and does it with a frightful love that plunges her into tears.

Pain enters the child's body. It is sharp at first. Then awful. Then contradictory. Like nothing else. Nothing: and it's when the pain becomes unbearable that it begins to go away, changes, becomes something good to moan at, scream at, takes over all of your body, your head, all of the strength in your body, your head, and in your totally defeated ability to think.

The suffering leaves her skinny body, it leaves her head. Her body remains open to the outside. It has been breached, it is bleeding, its suffering is over. This can't be called pain anymore, it might be called death.

And then the suffering leaves her body, leaves her head, imperceptibly leaves the whole surface of her body and disappears in the previously undiscovered happiness of loving without knowing.

She remembers. She is the last to remember. She still hears the sound of the sea in the room. And she remembers having written that. As she remembers the Chinese street. She even remembers writing that the sea was present that day in the lovers' room. She wrote the words: *the sea,* and three other words—the words *simply* and *beyond compare.*

The lovers' bed.
They may be sleeping. We don't know.
The noise of the city has returned. It is continuous, all of a piece. It is the noise of vast spaces.
Through the shutters, sunlight falls in patterns on the bed.
And there are bloodstains on the lovers' hands and bodies.
The child wakes up. She looks at him. He is sleeping in the cool breeze of the fan.

In the first book, she had said that the noise of the city was so close you could hear it rubbing against the shutters, like people walking through the room. That they were in that public noise, displayed there, *where the outside came inside the room.* She would again say it in a film, again, or in a book, again, she would always say it. And she says it again here.

You could also say here that the room keeps them "open" to the outdoor sounds banging on the shutters, the walls, to the people rubbing against the wooden shutters. To laughter. To errands and children shouting. To vendors hawking ice cream, watermelons, tea. And then, suddenly, to the sounds of that American music mixed with the panic whistle of trains across New Mexico, to the sounds of that desperation waltz, that sad and bygone sweetness, that despair at the happiness of the flesh.

She said she could still recall his face. Could still remember the names of the posts in-country, of the tunes that were popular then.

But his name she had forgotten. You, she said.

She had been told it again. And then she had forgotten it again. Later, she preferred still to suppress his name in the book and leave it forgotten forever.

She still saw the scene plainly in its distress, a wrecked ship—dead plants, the whitewashed walls of the room.

The canvas shade against the heat. The blood on the sheets. And the city, always invisible, always external—those things she remembered.

He wakes without moving. He is half asleep. Seen this way, he looks like a teenager. He lights a cigarette.

Silence.

He snuggles up to her, he doesn't speak to her. She points at the plants, she speaks in a low voice, under her breath, she smiles, and he, he says there's no point thinking about it, they've been dead a long time. He always forgets to water them. And he always will. He speaks in a low voice, as though the street could hear.

"You're sad."

She smiles and makes a slight gesture:

"I suppose so."

"It's because we made love during the day. It will pass when night falls."

He looks at her. She sees him. She lowers her eyes.

She looks at him, too. She sees him. She pulls back. She looks at his thin body, long, supple, perfect, with the same kind of miraculous beauty as his hands. She says:

"I've never seen anyone so handsome."

The Chinese looks at her as though she hadn't spoken. He looks at her, he focuses on that alone, looking at her to hold on to something afterwards of what he has before him, this white child. He says:

"You're probably a little sad all the time, aren't you . . ."

Silence. She smiles. She says:

"Always a little bit sad? Yes, maybe. I don't know . . ."

"It's because of your little brother . . ."

"I don't know . . ."

"Why else?"

"I don't know. That's me, that's how I am . . ."

"Is that what your mother says?"

"Yes."

"What does she say?"

"She says: Leave her alone. That's how she is, and she always will be."

He laughs. They don't speak.

He strokes her again. She goes back to sleep. He looks at her. He looks at this person who has come to him, this visitor fallen from the hands of God, this white child of Asia. His blood sister. His child. His love. He already knows it.

He looks at her body, her hands, her face, he touches. He breathes in her hair, her hands still stained with ink, her little girl breasts.

She is asleep.

He closes his eyes and with a magnificent, Chinese gentleness, he presses his body against the body of the white child and under his breath he says he has begun loving her.

She doesn't hear him.

He turns off the light.

The room is lit by the glow from the street.*

The bachelor quarters. This is another night, another day. He is sitting in the armchair. The low table beside him. He's

---

*Some pointers for a movie:

Shoot the room lit by the light from the street. Keep the sound on for these shots, but leave it at its normal level, along with the noise from the street—and the ragtime and the waltz. Shoot the sleeping lovers, The Book as Pulp Novel.

And shoot the weak, sorry light from the streetlamps.

wearing a black silk dressing gown, like in the movies, the provincial hero. We can see what he's watching:

Her—the child.

She is sleeping. She is turned toward the wall, away from him, naked, slim, skinny, delightful, the way a child is.

She wakes.

They look at each other.

And with that look, the mute exchange in that look, the love that had been held back until then enters the room.

He says:

"You fell asleep. I took a shower."

He goes to get her a glass of water. He looks at her until the tears come.

He looks at her constantly, he looks at everything about her. She gives him back the glass, he puts it on the table. He sits back down. He looks at her some more. She, she might want him to speak again, but she doesn't say so. She doesn't say anything. Once more, it is difficult to know what she might be thinking. He says:

"You're hungry."

She nods: she might be hungry. Yes, that might be it. She can't really tell. She says:

"It's too late to go out to eat."

"There are late-night restaurants."

She says:

"Fine with me."

They look at each other, then look away.

The scene moves extremely slowly.

She gets out of bed.

She goes to take a shower.

He comes over. He does it for her, he washes her the native way, with the flat of his hand, without soap, very slowly. He says:

"You have the rain skin of Asian women. Your wrists are delicate like theirs, too, and your ankles—it's funny, isn't it, how do you account . . ."

She says:

"I don't."

They smile at each other. Desire returns. They stop smiling at each other. He dresses her. And then looks at her again. Looks at her. She, she is already a part of the Chinese. She knows that, the child. She looks at him and, for the first time, she discovers that another place has always been there between her and him. Since their first glance. Another place that protects them, a sheer, inviolable space. A sort of far-off, childhood China—why not?—one that would protect them from all knowledge that might be foreign to it. And that is how she discovers that she, she protects him just as he himself does from events like adulthood, death, sadness at evening, the solitude of wealth, the solitude of misery that is born of love as much as desire.

She looks at everything, she explores the place, this room, this man, this lover, this night through the shutters. She says it is dark out. Through the shutters she gives a long look at the absent little brother who knows nothing, who will never know anything about a shared happiness.

She says it is dark out, that it is almost cold suddenly. She looks at him.

She can't control her distress, she says she wants to see her little brother that very evening, because he doesn't know how she is doing, because he is alone.

The lover came over to her, he pressed his body to hers. He says he knows what is bothering her at the moment—the despair, the suffering. He says it's like that sometimes at a certain hour of the night, the confusion, he knows how lost you can feel. But it's not serious. Everyone feels that way at night when they can't sleep. He says that they may be in love with each other, you can't tell right away.

And then he lets her cry.

And then she says maybe she's hungry.

She laughs with him. She says slowly:

"I've been loving you a long time. I'll never forget you."

He says he's already heard that somewhere—he smiles—he can't remember where. He says, maybe in France.

And then she looks at him. At length. His sleeping body, his hands, his face. And she tells him under her breath that he is crazy. As if she were saying she loved him.

He opens his eyes. He says he's hungry too. They get dressed. They go out. He has the car keys, he doesn't wake the chauffeur.

They drive through a deserted Cholon.

They walk past a standing mirror at the entrance to the restaurant.

She looks at herself. She sees herself. She sees the man's hat made of rosewood-colored felt with a wide black band, the down-at-the-heel black shoes with rhinestones, the overdone red lipstick from the ferry where they met.

She looks at herself—she has come up close to her reflection. She comes even closer. Doesn't quite recognize herself. She doesn't understand what has happened. Years later, she will understand: her face is already the ruin it will be for the rest of her life.

The Chinese stops. He puts his arm around the child and he looks at her, too. He says:

"You're tired . . ."

"No, that's not it. I've aged. Look at me."

He laughs. Then turns serious. Then he holds her face and he looks at her very closely. He says:

"It's true—overnight."

He closes his eyes. Maybe out of bliss.

From the depths of the restaurant comes the clash of Chinese cymbals, hard to imagine if you don't know what it is like. The Chinese asks that they be seated in another room.

They are shown into a little room reserved for the uninitiated. There you hear the music much less clearly. The tables have tablecloths. There are a fair number of Europeans, Frenchmen, English tourists. The menus are in French. The waiters yell the orders in Chinese for the kitchen staff.

The Chinese orders Peking duck with fermented bean sauce. The child orders a cold soup. She speaks the Chinese of Chinese restaurants, like a Vietnamese from Cholon, no worse.

She laughs suddenly in the ear of the Chinese. She strokes his face. She says:

"It's funny, it comes on all of a sudden, happiness, like anger."

They eat. She stuffs herself. The Chinese says:

"It's strange, you make me want to carry you off . . ."

"Where to?"

"To China."

She smiles and makes a face.

"The Chinese—I don't much like the Chinese. Did you know that?"

"I did."

She says she'd like to know how his father got so rich, how he did it. He says his father never talks about money, neither to his wife nor to his son. But he knows how it started. He tells the child the story:

"It started with the cubicles. He had three hundred of them built. He owns several streets in Cholon."

"That's where you get your bachelor quarters . . ."

"Yes. Of course."

She looks at him. She laughs. He laughs too. No doubt, out of happiness.

"You're an only child?"

"No. But I'm the only heir to the fortune. Because I am my father's first wife's son."

She doesn't really understand. He says he won't ever explain it to her, that it isn't worth the trouble.

"Where in China are you from?"

"From Manchuria, I already told you that."

"That's in the north, right?"

"In the far north. It snows there."

"The Gobi Desert, then, that isn't far from Manchuria."

"I don't know about that. Maybe. We must have another name for it. We left Manchuria when Sun Yat-sen proclaimed the Chinese republic. We sold all of our land and all of my mother's jewelry. We left for the south. I remember, I was five years old. She cried, she screamed, she lay down in the street, my mother; she wouldn't go on, she said that if she had to live without her jewelry she'd just as soon die . . ."

The Chinese smiles at the child.

"He has a real head for business, my father. But as I said, how and when he came up with the idea for the cubicles, I don't know. He has a real head for ideas, too."

The child laughs. He doesn't ask why she's laughing.

She says:

"Your father, afterward he bought back your mother's jewelry?"

"Yes."

"What kind was it?"

"Jade, diamonds, gold. It's always pretty much the same with the dowries of rich daughters in China. I can't really remember anymore, but there were emeralds in there, too."

She laughs. He says:

"Why does that make you laugh?"

"It's your accent when you talk about China."

They look at each other. And for the first time, they smile at each other. The smile lasts a long time. And he isn't afraid anymore.

We don't know one another, says the Chinese.

They smile at each other some more. He says:

"It's true—I can't quite believe you're here. What was I saying?"

"You were talking about the cubicles . . ."

"Those cubicles, they're like African huts, the straw huts in the villages. They're a lot less expensive than a house. And you rent them for a fixed price. There aren't any surprises. That's what the Indochinese prefer, especially when they come from the countryside. People are never left to fend for themselves there, they're never alone. They live in the arcade along the street. You must not destroy the customs of the poor. Half the inhabitants sleep in the open arcades. During the monsoon it's cool there, it's wonderful."

"It's true, it seems like a dream, to be sleeping outdoors. And to be all together, too, but separate at the same time."

She looks at him. She laughs. They keep laughing. He has become totally Chinese again. He is very happy, his happiness is joyous and serious at the same time, too strong, and fragile. They eat. They drink choum. He says:

"It makes me very happy that you can appreciate the cubicles."

In a film version, the camera would be on the child when the Chinese tells the story of China. He might be a "fanatic" about that history. There is a kind of madness in his obsession that pleases the child. He says, he asks:

"China has been closed to foreigners for centuries, you know that?"

No, she doesn't know that, she says she knows very little

about China. She says she knows a little, some of the names of the rivers and mountains, but, no, nothing else.

He can't keep from talking about China.

He tells her about the first opening of the border, it was the English who managed it in 1842. He asks:

"That you know?"

She doesn't know. Not a thing, she says, she doesn't know a thing. So he goes on:

"It started at the end of the Opium War. Then the war between the English and the Japanese in 1894 broke up China and forced out the Manchu kings. And the first republic is proclaimed in 1911. The emperor abdicates in 1912. And he becomes the first president of the republic. At his death in 1916, a period of anarchy sets in that ends with the Kuomintang in power and a victory for Sun Yat-sen's spiritual heir, Chiang Kai-shek, who currently rules China. Chiang Kai-shek is fighting the Chinese Communists? That you know?"

A little, she says. She listens to his voice, that other French spoken by China, she is filled with wonder. He goes on:

"It was after another war—I can't remember which—at the end, the Chinese finally understood they weren't alone on the earth. Except for Japan, they thought they were the only ones on the face of the earth, that China was everywhere. I forgot to tell you: for centuries, all the kings of China were Manchus. Until the last one. After that they weren't kings anymore, they were chieftains."

"Where did you learn all that?"

"It was my father, he taught me. And then, in Paris I read the dictionary."

She smiles at him. She says:

80

"I really like the French you speak when you talk about China . . ."

"I forget my French when I talk about China, I want to go fast, I don't want to be boring. I can't talk about Manchuria in this country, because here, the Chinese in Indochina, they're all from Hunan."

They get the check.

The child watches him pay. He says:

"You'll be late getting back to school."

"I get back when I want to."

The Chinese is discreetly astonished. Suddenly uneasy at the child's freedom. A sharp pain, just born, came into his eyes when he smiled at the child.

She looks at him silently. She says:

"You're desperate. You don't know it. You don't know how to be desperate. But I know it for you."

"Desperate about what?"

"About money. My family is desperate about money, too. It's the same for your father and my mother."

She asks him what he does at night. He says he goes and drinks choum with the chauffeur along the waterways. They chat. Sometimes the sun is rising when they get home.

What do they talk about? she asks. He says: "About life." He adds: "I tell my chauffeur everything."

"About you and me, too?"

"Yes, even about my father's fortune."

This is Lyautey Boarding School by night.

The courtyard is deserted. Over by the refectory, the young houseboys are playing cards. One of them is singing. The child stops, she listens to the songs. She knows the songs of Vietnam. She listens for a bit. She knows them all. The young houseboy from the paso doble crosses the courtyard, they wave to each other, smile at each other: Good evening.

All the dormitory windows are open because of the heat. The girls are shut in behind them in their white mosquito-netting cages. You can hardly make them out. The blue night-lights in the hallways make them look very pale, expiring.

Hélène Lagonelle asks in a low voice how things went—she says: "with the Chinese." She asks what he's like. The child says he's twenty-seven. He's skinny. He may have had a slight illness when he was small. But nothing serious. He doesn't work. If he were poor it would be awful, he could never make a living, he'd die of hunger—but he, he doesn't know that.

Hélène Lagonelle asks if he is handsome. The child pauses. The child says he is. Very, very handsome? Hélène asks. Yes. His soft skin, his golden color, his hands, everything. She says he is handsome all over.

"His body—how is it beautiful?"

"Like Paulo's will be in a few years."

So the child thinks.

Hélène says it may be smoking opium that takes away his strength.

"Maybe. Luckily, he's very rich, he doesn't work at all. It's his being rich that takes away his strength, too. All he does is

82

make love, smoke opium, play cards. He's a kind of millionaire delinquent, you know what I mean."

The child looks at Hélène Lagonelle. She says:

"It's funny, that's how I want him."

Hélène says that when the child talks about him, she, Hélène, wants him too, like her.

"When you talk about him, I want him that way, too."

"You want him a lot?"

"Yes. With you, together with you."

They kiss. Indecent until their tears still the songs of the young houseboys, who have come over to the dormitory stairs.

Hélène says:

"He's the one I want. He's the one. You know it. You wanted him."

"Yes. I still want him."

"It hurt a lot?"

"A lot."

Silence. Hélène asks:

"So much that it can't be compared to anything else, anything at all?"

"Anything at all. It's over very quickly."

Silence.

"Now you've lost your honor."

"Yes. It's done"—she laughs—"forever."

"The same as with a white."

"Yes. The same."

Silence. Hélène Lagonelle cries softly. The child doesn't notice it. Hélène says, sobbing:

"What about me, do you think I could stand it with a Chinese."

"If you have to ask yourself that question, the answer is no."

So Hélène tells the child not to pay attention to what she says, it's just the emotion.

She asks the child how she could do it. The child asks her: "How do you think?"

"I guess I thought it was because you were poor."

The child says, maybe. She laughs, touched. She says: "I want very much for it to happen to you. Very much. Especially with a Chinese."

Mistrustful, Hélène doesn't answer.

The young houseboys are still singing at the back of the courtyard over by the refectory. The girls listen to the songs in Vietnamese. They may be singing along with them softly in Vietnamese.*

The next morning.

Hélène Lagonelle says the racket they hear is the municipal water carts. Hélène Lagonelle says what they smell is the scent of the streets after they've been washed down, reaching as far as the school dorms.

She wakes the others, who yell at her to leave them in peace.

Hélène goes on. She says the scent is so fresh, it could even

---

*In a film version, this detail would recur every time the child came home at night. To add a touch of everydayness the film otherwise lacks, aside from the school schedule and the routine of sleep, showers, and meals.

be the Mekong. That in the end, this boarding school is almost like their birthplace.

After making her declaration, Hélène sings. She seems happy these days, Hélène Lagonelle, in love with the Chinese herself as she listens to the child from Sadec talk about him.

The child is walking along rue Lyautey. Slowly. The street is empty. She gets to school. She stops. Looks at the empty street. All the students have gone into class. There are no children left outside. You can hear the sound of other classes at recess in an interior courtyard.

The child stays outdoors, behind a column in the hallway.

She isn't waiting for the Chinese. It's something else: she doesn't want to go into school until recess is over. Suddenly, the bell sounds. She goes in, slowly reaches the place in the hallway where the students are waiting for the teacher to arrive.

The teacher arrives.
The students go in.
The teacher smiles at the daughter of the head of the Native School at Sadec.

The school hallway, empty.
The floor of the hallway is filled with sunlight partway up the wall.

We see the empty hallway again at the afternoon bell.

The sunlight has vanished from the floor.

Seen from behind, the child is leaving the school hallway.

Ahead of her, set back from the school door, the Chinese limousine. Only the chauffeur is there. When he sees the child, he gets out to open the door for her. She understands. She doesn't ask him any questions. She knows. The chauffeur carries her off to her lover. Delivers her to him. That suits her.

The camera remains focused on her the entire ride, as she looks out this evening, not seeing a thing.

Across the city. Two or three landmarks, right off the list: the Charner Theater, the Cathedral, the Eden Cinema, the Chinese restaurant for whites. The Continental, the most beautiful hotel in the world. And the river, that incantation, always, day or night, empty or crowded with junks, calls, laughter, songs, and sea birds coming up from the Plain of Reeds.

The Chinese opens the door before she knocks. He has on his black nighttime dressing gown. They stay where they are. He takes her bookbag, he throws it on the floor, he undresses her, stretches out next to her on the floor. Then waits. Waits. Some more. Says in a very low voice:

"Wait."

He enters the black night of the child's body. Stays there. Moans, crazed with desire, doesn't move, says under his breath:

"Not yet, wait . . ."

She becomes his object, secretly prostituted to him alone. Nameless now. Offered up like a thing, a thing he alone has stolen. Taken, used, penetrated by him alone. Something suddenly unknown, a girl child without identity except that she belongs to him, is his sole estate—there is no word for that—melded into him, absorbed in a totality that is itself just being born, called since the dawn of time by another, an unjust name: indignity.

We see them again *afterward,* lying on the floor in the same spot. They have become the lovers in the book.

The bed is empty. The lovers are still lying down. The fan rotates overhead. His eyes are closed. He feels for the child's hand. He finds it, keeps it in his own hand. He says:

"Last night I went to a whorehouse to make love with you again. I couldn't, I left."

Silence. She asks:

"If the police found us . . ."—she laughs—"I'm very underage . . ."

"They might jail me for two or three nights. I don't know. My father would pay, it wouldn't be serious."

The street in Cholon. The streetlamps go on in the twilight.

The sky is already evening blue, you can look at it without searing your eyes.

At the earth's edge the sun, on the verge of dying. It dies.

At the bachelor quarters.

Night has fallen. The sky is bluer and bluer, dazzling. The child is far from the Chinese, over by the fountain, stretched out in the cool water of the basin. She is telling the story of her life. The Chinese listens from far off, distractedly. He is already somewhere else, he has embarked on the pain of loving this child. He doesn't really know what she's talking about. She is putting all of herself into this story she's telling. She says to him that she often tells this story, and that she doesn't care if people don't listen to it. She says it doesn't matter even if he doesn't listen to it.

"It doesn't matter if you're not listening. You can sleep for all I care. I'm telling this story so I can write it later on. I can't keep from doing it. Someday I'll write it, my mother's life.* How they did her in. How it took her years to believe you could steal all of someone's savings and then never speak to her again, turn her away, say that she's crazy, that you've never seen her before, laugh at her, make people think she's run amok in Indochina.

---

*She kept her promise: *The Sea Wall*.

And have people believe it, and also be ashamed to be seen with her—I'll tell about that, too. For years we didn't see any whites. Whites, they were ashamed of us. She had just a few friends left, my mother. All of a sudden, everyone had deserted us."

Silence.

The Chinese:

"That's what makes you want to write this book . . ."

The child:

"It isn't that, exactly. It isn't my mother's failure. It's the idea that those people from the Land Registry won't all be dead, a few will still be alive to read the book and die reading it. My mother used to say: 'I can still see that day, the first day, I thought it was the most beautiful day of my life. I brought all my savings in a little bag, I can remember, I gave it to the Registry agents. And I thanked them. Thank you for selling me this wonderful plot between the mountains and the sea.'

"Afterwards, when the water rose for the first time, they said they had never, no, never seen her at the Land Registry in Kampot, that she had never, no, never filed for a concession. My mother always cried at that point in her story, and said she knew that she would cry about it till the day she died, and she always apologized to her children for it, but that there was nothing she could do against the vileness of that white colonial scum. She would say: 'And then, later, they wrote to the governor of Cambodia to say I had gone crazy and should be sent back to France.' But then, instead of dying, she started hoping again. She hoped for three more years. We, her children, we couldn't understand that. And then we started believing our mother was crazy, but without ever telling her. She started buying mangrove logs to shore up the dikes again. She borrowed money. She

89

bought more stones to shore up the embankments along the seed beds."

At this point in the story the child always cried.

"And then the sea rose up.

"And then she quit.

"It went on for maybe four years, no one really knows anymore how long. And then it happened: it was all over. She gave up. She said: It's all over. She said she was giving up. And then she did. She left.

"The tides flooded the rice paddies, the dikes got swept away.

"The upper rice paddy, she gave it to the servants, along with the house and the furniture."

The child smiles. She apologizes. Holds back her tears but it's no use. She's crying.

"I still can't accept my mother's life being like that. I never will."

The Chinese has begun to listen to all of the story the child is telling. He leaves her on her own, far off. Her he has forgotten.

He listened to the mother's story.

Silence. The child adds:

"We still go there once or twice a year, during the holidays, all four of us. Thanh, my mother, Paulo, and me. We drive all night. We get there by morning. We think we're going to stay, we can't, we head back the same night. She's at peace now, my mother. It's over. She's like she was before. Only she doesn't want anything anymore. She says her children are heroes to have put up with her. Her madness . . . herself. She says she doesn't expect anything anymore. Anything but death."

The child is still. She holds back her tears. She cries anyway.*

She used to say that it was the same the world over. That life was just that way.

The Chinese says:

"And you, you believe it, too."

"No. I only believe it for my mother. I absolutely believe it for the poor, but not for everyone."

"You believe it for Thanh."

"No. I believe the opposite for Thanh."

"What's the opposite?"

"I don't know yet. Only Thanh will know. He doesn't know yet that he knows, he doesn't know how to say it yet, but one day he will know how to say it and think it."

Of that the child is sure.

The Chinese asks her if she went to see the rice paddies after the last storm.

She says yes, they went, Paulo, Thanh, and herself. There was so much foam you couldn't make out a thing. The place had become engulfed in foam. There were mounds of it as far in as the mangroves along the shore, and on the mountain as well, even in the giant trees there was some.

---

*All her life, even into old age, she cried over the terrible injustice done their mother. She never got a penny back. The crooks from the French Land Registry were never reprimanded.

Silence. Then the child says:

"I didn't go to school today. I'd rather be with you. I didn't go yesterday, either. I'd rather be with you so we can talk."

The Chinese is standing.

He sits down in a chair.

He doesn't look at her anymore.

Suddenly the American music reaches them from the arcade along the cubicles: Duke Ellington's ragtime. Then there is that desperation waltz coming from someplace else, played on a piano in the distance—that will be the waltz that ends the film. So the return to France, still distant, already enters the lovers' room, and with it, the book.

The child and the Chinese listen to the waltz. The child says:

"He plays at the same time every day, probably when he comes home from work . . ."

"Probably. He moved into the cubicle a few weeks ago. I think he's a half-caste."

"It's always the same tune, like in a movie when the music comes up again and turns sad."

The Chinese asks where Thanh is from.

She says her mother found him one evening when she was coming back from the pepper plantations with her children, high in the mountains on the frontier between Siam and Cambodia.

They look at each other. They listen. She sits down beside him. The Chinese says:

"I'm going to buy records for when you've gone back to France."

92

"Yes."

The Chinese hides his face and whispers:

"For when you're dead—you might as well be."

"Yes."

They don't speak.

She leans against him.

She doesn't ask anything.

She says:

"It's true we're going to be separated forever. You thought we'd forgotten that?"

"No. Someday you're going home to France. Too much for me to bear. Someday I'll get married. I cannot, and I know that I will."

The child doesn't speak. It's as though she were ashamed for him.

The Chinese says:

"Come. Look at me."

He takes her face in his hand and forces her to look at him.

"You are going home when to France? Give me the date, right now."

"Before the school year's over. After my exams, but it isn't definite yet. She's having a lot of trouble leaving the colony, my mother. Every vacation she thinks she's going to leave, and then she stays. She says she's become a native finally—like us, Paulo and me. That there are a lot of colonials like her."

"And this year she will leave—you know it."

"Since she's asked to have her older son repatriated, this year she'll take a leave to go and see him. She can't live without him, she just can't . . ."

Silence. The Chinese says:

"I'll spend the rest of my life in this place, Sadec. Even if I travel, I'll always come back here. Because my fortune is here. For me, it's impossible to leave. Unless there's war."

The child looks at him. She doesn't understand. He says: "For years I've been engaged to a girl from Manchuria." The child smiles. She says she knows it.

"I'd heard. Thanh told me. Everyone knows everywhere, it's because of the little maids telling family secrets."

Silence. And the child says:

"I could listen to your stories about China a hundred times over . . ."

She takes his hands and puts them to her face, she kisses them. Asks him to tell her.

The Chinese tells her a story of imperial China, his eyes on her alone, the little white girl.

"We were chosen by our families, she as well as me, when we were children. I was seventeen years, she was seven years. That's how it is in China, in order to protect the family inheritance from ill fortune the two families have to have the same wealth; it's so much the Chinese way, we can't do otherwise anymore."

He looks at her:

"I'm boring you."

"No."

"We have children right away. Responsibilities. Mistresses. Very quickly there's nothing you can change about your life. Chinese men, even when they're not so wealthy, they have mistresses. The wives know it. That gives them peace: if the men have women on the outside, they always come home."

"China isn't the only place—"

94

"No, only in China is it so established."

"You're going to marry this fiancée."

"Yes," he says with a sob. "Not you. Never you. Never. Not even in the next life."

She cries into her hands. Seeing him cry makes her cry.

"If we hadn't met this way, if I had been a rich Chinese woman, that's how it would have gone. So maybe it comes back to the same thing . . ."

He looks at her. He doesn't answer. He says:

"Maybe it comes back to the same thing, I don't know yet. Come over here."

She comes over to him on the bed, she lies down. She touches his forehead. She says:

"You're hot."

He looks at her with all his strength. He says:

"I feel it very deeply, telling you these things—that's why."

With his hands, he bares the child's face to see it whole. She says:

"I would have liked for us to marry. To be married lovers."

"To make each other suffer."

She isn't smiling anymore.

She's crying. And at the same time, she tells him what happiness would have been like:

"Yes, for that, to make each other suffer as much as possible. And to come back afterward."

Silence. She says:

"Soon your wife will hear our story, through all the little maids at Sadec. And she will suffer. Maybe she knows already. The suffering I'm causing you both is another way you will be married."

"Yes."

He says:

"The families expect the first child, the heir, right from the first night. I'm very worried about that, about not being able to."

She doesn't answer. She says:

"After that, you'll take a trip around the world."

"Yes. That's true. At that point you will still be on the boat to France."

Silence. She asks:

"On the boat—where?"

"In the Indian Ocean. Off Colombo."

"Why there?"

"I just picked a place."

Silence. And the Chinese says:

"We're going to go to Long-Hai. I've rented a room at the Bungalow de France."

"For when?"

"Whenever you want. Today. Tonight."

"And what about school?"

The Chinese suddenly switches to the formal *vous*:

"That doesn't matter. You never go to school everyday, even before. You go to the zoo often. I made some inquiries."

The child pulls back a little. She is afraid. She asks, she cries out in a low voice:

"But why go to Long-Hai, why there?"

The Chinese looks straight at her and his eyes close under the weight of the awful thought of losing the child. He says:

"I've begun suffering over parting with you. I'm going mad. I can't part with you, it's not possible, and I will do it, I know it."

He doesn't look at her anymore. With his eyes closed, he

strokes her hair. She pulls away again, she gets up, goes over to the other door. He asks:

"Why don't you like Long-Hai?"

"My family went there, and once I was frightened. It's awful. The tigers come to swim at night at Long-Hai, and once, one morning, with my little brother, we saw fresh tiger tracks, a little tiger, but just the same; we ran off, we were so scared. And also, the beach is completely deserted, there's nothing there, not a village, not a . . . nothing, nobody . . . there's nothing but madmen, beggars, they go begging at the pagodas . . ."

The child closes her eyes. She is pale. The Chinese comes over to her.

"What is it you're most scared of? Tigers or people?"

She says, she yells it:

"The people. You. You, the Chinese."

A long silence from him whom she suddenly no longer recognizes. He asks:

"They come from where, those people?"

"From Annam. From the islands in the Bay of Along. From the coasts. A lot from that penitentiary, you know—Poulo Condore. Crazies, madmen pass through, too. And women who've been banished from the villages. In the pagodas, they give them hot rice and tea, sometimes they kill a stray dog and they cook it on the beach, those people, and it smells very bad a hundred miles down the beach."

"Those places, they're also the Chinese invasion routes."

"Could be. I wouldn't know about that. I thought they came through the Hunan mountains, the Chinese."

She says that among all those people it's the women who are the scariest. Because they laugh while they're crying.

"Where do they come from?"

This the child doesn't really know. Now she's making it up. All of it. She says they come from India by sea, those women. They hide in junks. They've completely lost their minds, they're all crazed with fear, from their children having died of hunger, from the sunlight, the forest, the clouds of mosquitoes, the mad dogs, and the tigers, too. The Chinese says there's one of those beggarwomen between Vinh-Long and Sadec at night who shrieks while she's laughing, haranguing, singing. Scaring you.

The child says she knows that beggarwoman, like everyone else between Sadec and Vinh-Long: she's from Laos, it's Laotian lullabies she's singing.

He laughs. He says:

"You're making it up. How do you know that?"

The child is scared. Is she lying? She no longer knows how she knows that, she doesn't know if she's lying or not. She says:

"I think, from Anne-Marie Stretter. She knows Laotian, she comes from Laos, she recognized the Laotian words in the songs. She talked to my mother about it once at the Club—so there."

The child sings the whole first verse the Ganges beggar-woman sings on the post road by night. She says:

"You see, I know that lullaby . . ."

He says that doesn't prove anything. He laughs. He asks:

"Who told you all that stuff about Long-Hai?"

"My mother, and Dô, and Thanh, too. They always have, always."

"Why do they tell you that?"

"To get me interested, why do you think they do . . ."

"Your mother doesn't go to the Club, because she's embarrassed about your older brother. And Mme. Stretter, you don't know her—neither your mother nor you. You're talking through your hat."

The child suddenly cries:

"Anyone can see her, Mme. Anne-Marie Stretter. She's out on her terraces every evening with her daughters. Who do you think she is, Mme. Stretter? First of all, everyone knows what happened to her in Laos, in Vientiane with that young man, it was in the newspapers."

The Chinese listens to her. He worships her. The child goes on with the story.

"And what's more, one day I saw her at a Latin lesson at the priest's in Vinh-Long. He was teaching the French children Latin and she, she came in with her daughters. She asked the priest who I was. He said: the daughter of the head of the girls' school. She smiled at me. She told the priest that was quite a look I had. I heard her. I told my mother. The next day my mother took me to Dr. Sambuc's clinic to find out if I'd have a squint later on. They reassured her, there was nothing like a squint there . . ."

"And did you learn Latin?"

"Well, a little. And then I dropped it."

Silence.

"No one's ever asked to marry you? It's the fashion in Saigon . . ."

"Of course. First my mother says yes right away, and then I cry, so she says no and everyone gets upset. The last one was a man at the Messageries Maritimes, he had to be at least thirty-five, thirty-eight years old. He made a lot of money. She almost gave in, my mother, but I said no, he was too fat, too red, you know . . ."

Silence. Then the Chinese asks:

"You were scared just now."

"Yes. You too."

"Yes."

"How would you have killed me at Long-Hai?"

"Like a Chinese. With cruelty on top of the killing."

He comes to get her over by the door. She seems drained. He carries her to the bed. She closes her eyes to sleep, she doesn't sleep. He takes her in his arms. He talks to her in Chinese. That makes her laugh every time.

"Sing to me in Chinese, too."

He sings in Chinese. Then he cries. She cries with him without knowing why.

They don't look at one another. Then she pleads with him. So he enters her with a gentleness she doesn't know yet. Then he stays there without moving. Their desire makes them moan. She closes her eyes. She says:

"Take me."

Whispering, the Chinese asks her:

"You'll tell me when you know your departure date."

"No."

She asks him for it again. He takes her.

She turns over, snuggles up to him. He embraces her. He says she is his child, his sister, his love. They don't smile at one another. He has put out the light.

"How would you have killed me at Long-Hai? Tell me again."

"Like a Chinese. With cruelty on top of the killing."

She declaims the end of the phrase as she would a poem.

The lycée—the halls are full of students. The child is waiting against a column in the hall. She is isolated, facing outward.

The assistant principal passes by, touches her shoulder. He says:

"I'd like a word with you."

She follows the assistant principal into his office.

"All right . . . Of course the students' mothers have forbidden their daughters to have anything to do with you. You know that . . ."

The child smiles. She knows it.

"But it's worse than that. The students' mothers have informed the head of Lyautey that you aren't sleeping regularly at the boarding school." A slight irritation on the assistant principal's part. "How they found out, I don't know. You've been caught"—he smiles—"in the dragnet of the mothers of the students of Saigon. They want their daughters to keep to their own kind. They say"—listen to this—"'Why does she need a baccalaureate, that little tart? Middle school is enough for people like her . . .'"

Silence. She asks:

"You're warning me because of my mother."

"Of course. You know how much I respect her." Pause. "Now, in your opinion, what can we do?"

"We can just draw it out. You go on warning me, and I go on not spending the night at Lyautey. I don't know—what do you think?"

Silence.

"I really don't know."

The assistant principal says:

"The head of Lyautey has notified your mother . . ."

"Sure. But my mother doesn't give a damn about our reputation—our family isn't like other families."

"What does she want for her children, your mother?"

"She wants them settled. So she can die. But she doesn't know that's what she wants."

The assistant principal goes on playing his role:

"You've also been skipping school, but I take care of that."

"I knew it."

The assistant principal looks at her affectionately.

"You and I—we're friends . . ."

The child smiles. She is less sure of it than he is.

"Really?"

The assistant principal confirms it:

"Really."

She smiles.

Silence.

"This is your last year in Indochina . . ."

"Yes. Possibly my last few weeks. Even if the principal

wants to expel me, it doesn't matter anymore. But I know he won't."

"No, he won't do that."

The assistant principal smiles at the child.

"I do appreciate your faith in us. 'It's the teaching profession that will have saved Indochina from white stupidity.' Your mother said that to me one day. I've never forgotten it."

The girl seems preoccupied, indifferent to affront throughout the conversation. She says:

"I don't think my mother cares about any of that now. She's had them repatriate her oldest son. Nothing else matters to her now."

The assistant principal didn't know.

"Oh, so she finally did it . . ."

"Yes."

"That's too bad. Such a charming boy, Pierre. You know, I met him when he was little."

Of course she knew it. The child's eyes fill with tears. He sees it:

"He was horrible to you and your little brother . . ."

The bell for the start of class. The assistant principal and the girl leave the office together. She asks:

"You knew my mother in Tonkin . . ."

He is surprised; she has never spoken about her family.

"Yes. You weren't born yet."

"What was she like? I really don't know."

He is surprised, he answers gracefully:

"Green eyes. And black hair. Lovely. Very cheery, fun-loving, very engaging. Delightful."

"Maybe too delightful?"

"Maybe . . ."

"And my father?"

"He was mad about her. Other than that, he was . . . an outstanding teacher."

The child knows her mother's life story. She has often talked with her about it. She says:

"I think she was happy with him all the same."

"I wouldn't doubt that. People spoke of her as a woman who had everything. But you can never tell." He turns toward the child, he repeats: "Never."

He adds: "It's true. I was about to say—go on doing whatever you want with your life, don't take anyone's advice."

She smiles. She says:

"Not even yours?"

He smiles with her. He says:

"Not even mine."

The bachelor quarters.

The Chinese says:

"I'm going to Sadec tonight, I have to, I'll be back in two days. The chauffeur will bring you your meal. We will take you back to the boarding school before leaving."

They shower. She tells him about her isolation at school. She laughs:

104

"They don't talk to me at school anymore because of you."

"You're imagining it."

"No. Some of the students' mothers have complained."

He laughs with her. He asks her what they're afraid of. She says:

"Syphilis. Plague. Mange. Cholera. The Chinese."

"Why the Chinese?"

"The Chinese—they haven't been colonized. Here they're the way they would be in America, they travel. You can't catch them to colonize them, and that upsets people."

The Chinese laughs. She laughs with him, she looks at him, blinded by the truth of it:

"You're right. It's nonsense. Nonsense."

Silence.

"Tonight I'm going back to the dormitory. They've notified my mother, too . . ."

The chauffeur brings in the tray. He puts it down on the table. Grilled meats and soup. They eat. And they talk. They talk to each other. They look at each other.

The Chinese smiles:

"We're tired. That's nice."

"Yes. And we were hungry, we didn't know it."

"Talking is nice, too."

"Yes. Do you talk with people sometimes?"

He smiles like a child. She looks at him. She says she will never forget him. He says:

"I used to talk a lot with my mother."

"What about?"

"About life."

They laugh.

She looks at him. She asks:

"Do you look like her?"

"People have said so. Me, I wouldn't know. She went to university in America, my mother, I didn't tell you that. Law, that's what she studied. To be an attorney."

"Your father didn't want her to . . ."

"No. She didn't want it either, anymore, she wanted to be with him all day long. They went around the world after their wedding."

Silence.

The child muses. She says:

"Maybe your mother would have liked me."

The Chinese smiles.

"Maybe. She was jealous, but maybe . . ."

"You think of her sometimes."

"Everyday, I imagine."

"She died when?"

"Ten years ago, I was seventeen, from the plague, it took two days, here, in Sadec."

He laughs and cries at the same time. He says:

"You see . . . I didn't die of grief."

She cries with him. He says she was funny, too, his mother, very cheery.

In the courtyard at Lyautey, Hélène Lagonelle is waiting for her friend. She is stretched out on that same bench facing the gate, in the dark part of the courtyard.

"Where were you . . ."

"With him."

Silence. Hélène Lagonelle was uneasy. That constant fear of being abandoned. She is still afraid. She undoes the child's braids. She smells her hair. She says:

"And you didn't go to school, either."

"We stayed at his bachelor quarters."

Silence. Hélène Lagonelle says with relish:

"One of these days it'll all blow up. You'll be expelled from school, from the boarding school—from everywhere."

The child says the idea of that happening someday thrills her.

"And what about me?"

"You," says the child, "I'll never, never, ever forget you . . ."

Hélène Lagonelle says there's been a phone call. That it was bound to come:

"They told me to tell you, you have to go see the counselor on duty. They said it's urgent. She's a Chinese half-caste. She's nice—our age."

The child went to see the young counselor.

The counselor is young and pleasant. The child says:

"You wanted to see me."

"Yes. You know why I . . . through Hélène . . ." She continues: "We've had to notify your mother. Since they called from the lycée. The assistant principal . . ."

107

The child isn't surprised. She laughs. She says she hadn't given it much thought. She says:

"There was no point notifying my mother. She knows all about it, and it's all the same to her. She must have forgotten. She pretends she believes in discipline, but she doesn't. She couldn't care less, my mother. I see her as a kind of queen, you know: a queen without a country, a queen of—what am I trying to say—of poverty, of madness, you know . . ."

The counselor sees the child doesn't know she's crying. She says:

"I know your mother's story. Of course, you're right. But she's a great teacher, too. They worship her in Indochina because she's so dedicated to her profession. She has educated thousands of children . . ."

"What do people say about her?"

"They say she has never given up on a child, not until he could read and write. She would hold classes late into the evening for children she knew would someday be workers, 'manual labor,' or as she put it: the exploited. She wouldn't let them go until she was sure they could read a work contract."

The child says that when students lived too far away to go home in the evening, she had them sleep at her house on mats in the living room, or in the school's playroom. The child says it was wonderful, those students all over the house . . .

The young counselor studies the child. Without any embarrassment, she says:

"You're the one with the Chinese lover . . ."

"Yes, that's me."

They smile at each other. The young counselor says:

"They're talking about it in all the schools. This is the first time it's happened."

"Why is that, do you suppose?"

·"I think it's the Chinese—the old Chinese who don't want to see white women with their sons, even as mistresses."

"And how did it happen in your case?"

"My father was white, a customs agent. And yours?"

"A teacher. A math teacher."

They laugh like a couple of students.

The counselor says:

"Your mother is going to have to come see the director. I'll be in trouble otherwise. I have to ask you to do it . . ."

The child promises.

It is very early morning. The mother must have traveled through the night with Thanh.

The mother crosses the empty courtyard. She heads for the office where the young counselor was the night before. She has on her old, gray cotton stockings, her old black shoes, her old hair is pulled back under her colonial helmet, and there is that enormous old handbag her children have always seen her with. And she still wears mourning for their father, thirteen years later—the black crêpe band on the white helmet.

An old lady, also French, receives the mother. She's the

head of Lyautey. They know each other. They had both arrived in Indochina when the education program for native children was beginning, in 1905, with the first groups of teachers coming from France. The mother talks about her daughter:

"She's a child who has always had her freedom, otherwise she would be running away constantly. Even I can't do anything about it, her own mother. If I want to keep her, I have to let her be free."

They've placed each other, they suddenly start using the familiar *tu*. They both come from the north, from Pas de Calais. The mother talks about her life.

"You may not know it, but my girl gets good grades in school, even while she's so free. What happened with my older son is so terrible, so awful, I'm sure you've heard about it, everyone knows everything here—having my girl get an education is my last hope."

The director had heard people talk about the child at teachers' meetings at Chasseloup-Laubat Secondary School.

The mother went on to tell her about the father's death, the ravages of amebic dysentery, the disaster of a family without a father, about her own problems, her profound confusion, her loneliness.

The director had cried with the mother. She had let the child live on at the boarding school the way she would at a hotel.

The mother came out of the director's office. She recrossed the courtyard. The child saw her. She looked at her, she didn't go over to her, ashamed of her mother. She went back into the dormitory, she hid and she cried over this mother of hers who wasn't the way she should be and who embarrassed her. The mother she loved.

This is a hallway at the lycée. It's raining. All the students are in the enclosed playground inside the second courtyard. The child is alone under the arcade that runs between the two courtyards. She is being shunned. She wants it that way, to be in that place. She looks at the rain falling in the big empty courtyard.

We can hear the sound of the others playing in the distance, at the other end of the arcade, cut off from her for as long as she lives—she can sense it. She already knows, the child, that they will be separated from one another for the rest of their lives, the way they already are in the present. She doesn't ask why. She only knows that is how it is.

Today, the car of the Chinese is in front of the school. The chauffeur is alone. He gets out and speaks to the child in French:

"He has gone to Sadec again, the young master. His father, he is ill."

He says he has orders to take her back and forth between school and the dormitory during his master's absence.

At Lyautey, the young houseboys are singing in the court-yards. And Hélène Lagonelle is asleep.

The next day, at the same spot in the street by the school, the chauffeur is no longer alone. The young master is there in the car. School is letting out. The child goes over to him. Without a word, in front of passersby, students, they come together in a very long kiss, oblivious of everything.

The Chinese says:
"He's going to live, my father. He has refused, he says he'd rather see me dead."

The Chinese has been drinking choum. The child doesn't understand any of what he's telling her. The child doesn't tell him that. She listens carefully. She knew nothing about the real reasons why the Chinese took this trip, he talks to her in the poor French of the Chinese from the colony when they've been drinking choum. He says:
"I beg him. I tell him he must have had a love like this sometime in his life, that it's not possibly otherwise. I ask him to marry you for a year, and then send you back to France. Because it's not yet possible for me already to give up this love for you."

The child is silent, then she asks where it was, this conversation with the father. The Chinese says it was in the father's

112

room, in that house in Sadec. The child wants to know where the father stands when they talk. The Chinese says the father is on a cot all day long because he is old, noble, and wealthy. But that before, he would receive people in his American office. That he—this father's son—he almost always cast himself at his feet when listening to him.

The child feels like laughing, but she doesn't laugh.

The Chinese tells the child about it, still in faulty French. But what the child hears is the father's story, through his words, his answers. The Chinese goes on:

"I tell him it is too new, too strong, I tell him that it is awful for me to separate me from you like that. That he, my father, he must know what it is like, a love like that, so great that it never happens ever again in life, ever."

The Chinese cries as he says these words: ever again in life, ever. He says:

"But my father, he doesn't give a damn about anything."

The child asks whether the father has ever felt the kind of love he talked about. The Chinese doesn't know. He thinks about it, tries to remember. At last he says yes, probably. It was when he was very young, that girl from Canton, a student, too.

The child asks if he has ever spoken with him about her. The Chinese says:

"Never with anyone. Except with my mother," he adds, "but after the affair had ended. So it was my mother who suffered over it."

The Chinese is silent.

The child closes her eyes, she sees the river in front of the villa with the blue tiles. She says there was a stairway with steps going down into the river. He says that the steps are still there for the poor women and their children to bathe in the waters of the river and wash their clothes, that the steps go down until they disappear. And that his father settled on a cot facing this stairway so he could watch the women undressing and going into the waters of the river and laughing together. And he, his son, the little Chinese, he had watched them with him when he was old enough to see such things.

The Chinese said his father had given him an unsealed letter to read, it was addressed to her mother. He had read it and given it back to his father. He claimed to have forgotten what this letter to her mother said. The child didn't believe him. The child said she would probably never see the steps and the women going down into the river again, but she would remember them now for the rest of her life.

And then the Chinese remembered a second letter that his father had written to him, his son, and that he had lost and then found it again, though he thought he had given it back to his father along with the one addressed to her mother. The Chinese took it out now and translated it for the child:

"I can't allow what you are asking of me, your father. You know that. After the year you're asking me for, it is utterly impossible for you to give her up. And then you lose your wife-to-be and her dowry. Out of the question for her to love you after that. So I am keeping the dates the families have set."

The Chinese goes on translating the father's letter:

"I know the circumstances of this girl's mother. You must find out how much she needs to settle her debts for the sea walls. I know this woman. She is respectable. She was robbed by the French officials at the Land Registry in Cambodia. And she has a bad son. I've never seen the little girl. I didn't know there was a daughter in the family."

The child says she doesn't understand a thing in the father's letter. She holds back her laughter, then she can't hold it back anymore and laughs very hard. And suddenly the Chinese laughs with her.

The Chinese takes his father's letter back from the child's hands and finishes reading it:

"In a few days, I will know their departure date. You must go to see her mother this very day to settle the money issue. After that, it will be too late. You must be very polite to her. Very respectful, so she isn't ashamed to take the money."

When the Chinese reaches the mother's house, two Chinese are already waiting, sitting on the ground against the wall. They're the owners of La Fumerie du Mékong. The three Chinese recognize one another.

The older son is sitting at the dining room table. He seems not to understand what is going on, almost as though he were sleeping. He already has the pallor of opium users, their sunken, blood-red lips.

The little brother is there, too—Paulo. He is stretched out against the dining room wall. He is a teenager, good-looking the way half-castes are. He and the Chinese smile at each other. The little brother's smile recalls his young sister's. Beside the little brother there is another very handsome young man, that's the mother's little chauffeur, the one they call Thanh. He looks like the little brother and the sister, though it's hard to say how: possibly the very pure, innocent fear in his glance.

The scene is frozen. No one moves. No one talks. No one says hello.

The three Chinese say a few words with great composure.

And then they fall silent.

The Chinese lover goes over to the older brother and explains:

"They say they're going to file a complaint against you. They're the owners of La Fumerie du Mékong. You don't know them. You only know the managers, who are employees."

No answer from the older brother.

The mother appears, she has just taken a shower, she is barefoot, in a loose dress Dô has cut for her from a sampot made of local cloth, her hair is wet, uncombed. The little brother is still sitting against the wall, away from the center of the scene, apparently taking an interest in what is going on, this sudden coming and going of strangers in the house.

The Chinese looks at the mother with passionate curiosity.

She smiles at him. It's in her smile that he sees the resemblance to her daughter. The little brother has the same smile.

The mother attaches no significance to the presence of a third Chinese in the house, even a chic one, dressed European-style. For her, all Chinese come from the opium dens. She asks her older son:

"How much do you owe?"

"Ask them. In any case, they're slime, they'll lie."

The mother recognizes a Chinese she's never seen before:

"Is what my son says true, Monsieur?"

The Chinese:

"It's true, Madame." Smiling, he adds: "Forgive me, but they won't back down, ever. They'll stop you from getting on the boat. If you want to get rid of them, you'd do best to pay up."

The mother realizes that "the third Chinese" is not a creditor. She smiles at him.

The Chinese talks to his compatriots in Chinese. They depart immediately when they realize he is the son of the Chinese from the blue house.

The older brother asks the Chinese stranger:

"What are you here for?"

The Chinese turns to the mother. His answer is for her:

"You asked to see me, Madame."

The mother tries to place him:

"Who are you? I don't remember . . ."

"You don't remember . . . it's about your daughter . . ."

The older brother laughs at the joke.

The mother asks:

"What has happened to my daughter?"

The Chinese doesn't lower his eyes. He smiles at the mother. There's a kind of playful insolence about him that day, a self-assurance he gets from being there, in that house for

117

whites, regardless of how poor the whites are, and from the interest the mother shows in him, the way she smiles at him, looks at him. He answers:

"I thought you knew—I'm having an affair with her."

Silence. The mother is surprised, but only mildly.

"Since when?"

"Two months now. Didn't you know?"

She looks at her son. She says:

"Yes and no. You see, I've been through so much . . ."

The older brother:

"Everyone knows. What do you want?"

"I don't want anything. It's you, Madame. You sent my father a letter. You told him you wanted to see me."

She looks at her son, there's a question in her glance. The older son says:

"I'm the one who wrote it. The letter is very clear—your father didn't tell you what we wanted?"

The Chinese ignores the son. He speaks to the mother:

"My father doesn't want a marriage between his son and your daughter, Madame. But he is prepared to give you the money you need to settle your debts and leave Indochina."

The older brother says:

"Is it because she's been dishonored that your father doesn't want you married?"

The Chinese looks at the brother in silence and says with a smile:

"Not just that. Also because she's not Chinese."

The mother says:

"And because she's poor . . ."

118

The Chinese smiles as though this were a game:

"Yes. And young a little. A little too young, too, but that's the least important. The Chinese in China also like very young girls."

Silence. Then the Chinese says why he has come:

"My father tells me, Madame, that he is prepared to pay a certain sum of money to try to repair the injury I've done your family."

The older brother:

"How much?"

The Chinese acts as though he hasn't heard.

The mother is overwhelmed, she moans suddenly. The Chinese smiles at her. The mother says:

"But, Monsieur—how can you expect me, Monsieur, to come out with it just like that. How can you calculate a thing like that—dishonor?"

"You don't need to calculate anything like that, Madame. You need only state the sum you would like to have."

The mother laughs, the Chinese too. She laughs hard, she says:

"Everything, Monsieur. Look at me. I look like absolutely nothing, and I have the debts of a head of state."

They laugh together, clearly in sympathy. The older brother is alone.

The Chinese says:

"Obviously, I will never be able to give you as much as you would have had if your daughter had become my wife, Madame . . ."

"How much would it have been—say it, Monsieur, just to see . . ."

"I don't really know, Madame. It would have been considerable. What with the real estate, the gold, the securities. But I can still help you out. He laughs—"Forgive me.""

The mother is in a tizzy for the Chinese.

"But how, Monsieur? How can I do it?"

The Chinese, smiling:

"I can lie, steal from my father."

Almost under his breath in the distance, the brother is cursing him.

"Swine . . ." To his mother: "Don't let that swine fool you. He's playing with you, can't you see that?"

Neither the mother nor the Chinese pay any attention to the older brother. The mother is completely taken up in her discovery of the Chinese, her little girl's lover. And now she forgets her difficulties, her troubles, she starts smiling at him, forgetting her own fate, and discovering what lies beyond her story, the existence of this Chinese with his sweet and mocking air. His visit charms her. Life charms her. As though she were in a chic salon, she says:

"Monsieur—can it be your father has no heir other than yourself?"

"He does. But I am the oldest son of my father's first wife. By Chinese law, I am the sole heir to his fortune—to avoid breaking up the inheritance."

Her interest drawn by the law, the mother reflects:

"Oh, I knew that. Yes, before, yes, yes—what you say is true. You couldn't get around the law? Persuade your father to . . ."

The Chinese laughs sympathetically.

120

"Now, that—just the idea makes me laugh, Madame, forgive me."

"They're terrible, aren't they, the old Chinese?"

The Chinese smiles, he says they really are terrible, but very generous sometimes, too.

The mother could listen to him forever, this Chinese. He says:

"I could kill him, perhaps, but convince him to violate the law, no. But depend on me, Madame, one way or another, I will help you."

They look at each other. They smile at each other. The older brother seems disheartened. The Chinese comes over to the mother. He smiles at her. He speaks to her—in front of people he doesn't know. She listens, passionately, like her child, the mother; she even has the same very direct look.

The Chinese says:

"I won't rob my father, Madame. I won't lie to him. I won't kill him. I was making up stories because I wanted to get to know you—for her sake, for your daughter. The truth is, my father is inclined to help you, and he will get money to you through me. I have a letter from him promising me that. I would have to do what I told you only if the sum weren't sufficient." The mother smiles. "But for my father, it will under no circumstances be a question of money, but rather of time, of the bank, of what is right, you understand . . ."

The mother says she feels completely sure of that.

He stops talking. They look at each other with feeling. And behind that smile, following that smile, she sees the Sadec heir's barely visible despair.

"If I married your daughter, my father would disown me, and then it would be you, Madame, who wouldn't want your child to marry a poor Chinese man."

The mother laughs.

"That's so true, Monsieur. There's that, too, that's how life is, full of contradictions . . ."

Together they laugh about life.

In the silence that falls, the mother says in a very low voice:

"You love that child so much . . ."

She doesn't expect an answer. She senses despair, fear on the lips, in the eyes of the Chinese. She says, barely audibly:

"Forgive me . . ."

The mother is beginning to forget about the question of the money. The mother's interest in everything that happens everywhere, in her own life and anyone else's, just as much—that is what brings the Chinese back to the child. To be more precise, he rediscovers the reflection of the child's curiosity in the way the mother listens to him.

The mother says sweetly:

"You speak good French, Monsieur."

"Thank you, Madame. And you, if you will allow me, you have been charming to me."

The older brother yells:

"That's enough of that now. We'll let you know how much we want through my whore of a sister."

The Chinese acts precisely as though the older brother didn't even exist. He suddenly becomes terribly calm and kind.

And the mother, without meaning to, remains with the Chinese. She asks him:

"My daughter knows all about this?"

122

"Yes. But she doesn't know I've come to see you yet."

"And what do you think she would say if she knew . . ."

"I don't know, Madame."

The Chinese smiles. He says:

"First she'd get angry . . . perhaps. And then all of a sudden she wouldn't care, just so long as you got the money." He smiles: "You have a regal daughter, Madame."

The mother lights up with happiness, she says:

"What you're saying, it's so true, Monsieur."

They part.

These are the bachelor quarters.

It is night.

The Chinese has returned from Sadec.

The child is in bed, she isn't asleep.

They look at each other without speaking. The Chinese sits down in the armchair, he doesn't go over to the child. He says:

"I've been drinking choum, I'm drunk."

He cries.

She gets up, she goes to him, she undresses him, she pulls him over to the fountain. He lets her. She showers him with rainwater. She strokes him, she kisses him, she talks to him. He cries with his eyes closed, alone.

In the street the sky lights up, the night is already nearly day. In the room, it is still very dark.

He says:

"Before you, I didn't know anything about suffering. I thought I knew, but I knew nothing."

He repeats: nothing.

She pats his body lightly with the towel.

She says to herself, under her breath:

"This way you'll be less hot. What you really need is not to dry off at all . . ."

He cries very softly, without wanting to. He insults the child, lovingly, as he cries.

"A cheap little white girl I found in the street. That's what she is. I should have suspected as much."

He stops talking, and then he looks at her and he starts in again:

"A little whore, a little nothing . . ."

She turns away to laugh. He sees her and he laughs too, together with her.

She soaps him. She bathes him. He lets her. Their roles are reversed.

It makes her feel good to do that. She's protecting him here. She leads him over to the bed, he knows nothing, he says nothing, he does what she wants him to. That makes her feel good. She has him stretch out beside her. She slips beneath his body, covers herself with his body. Stays there, motionless, happy. He says:

"I can't do it with you anymore. I thought I still could. I can't anymore."

Then he dozes off. Then he starts talking again. He says:

"I'm dead. I'm desperate. Maybe I'll never make love again. Never be able to again."

124

She looks at him very closely. She wants him very much. She smiles:

"Would you like that, never to make love again?"

"Right now, yes, I would like . . . to keep all the love for you even after you leave and forever."

She takes his face in her hands. She squeezes it. He cries. His face trembles from time to time, the eyes close and the mouth tightens. He doesn't look at her. She says softly:

"You've forgotten me."

"It's the pain I'm in love with. I don't love you anymore. It's my body, it doesn't want anything to do with her, the one who's leaving."

"Yes. When you speak, I understand it all."

He opens his eyes. He looks at the child's face. Then he looks at her body. He says:

"You don't even have breasts . . ."

He takes the child's hand and he puts it on her own sex.

"You do it. For me. To show me what's in your head."

She does it. They look at each other while she does it. He calls her my little girl, my child, and then in a flood of words he says things in Chinese, angry and despairing.

She calls to him. She has placed her mouth over his and she calls to him:

"You lousy little Chinese, you little crook . . ."

They pull away from each other. They look at each other. He says:

"It's true, sometimes I even want to kill my own father."

He also says:

"Nothing else will happen in my life except this love for you."

They are motionless on the bed, entwined, but separated from each other by his closed eyes, his silence.

She gets out of bed. She walks around the bachelor quarters. She goes far from him, over by the second door, the one "to escape by," hides from him. She is frightened. She stops. She doesn't look, she is frightened again in that way she began to be a few days ago and which she can't control. Scared of being killed by *this stranger* from the trip to Long-Hai.

She talks to him as she walks. She says:

"You shouldn't regret it. You remember, you told me I would always move on, would never be true to anyone."

He says that even that doesn't matter to him now. Everything is behind, he says. The child likes this word, but she doesn't quite understand what he means by that expression. Behind what? she asks him. He says he doesn't know what, either. All the same, he's saying it because it is the right word.

She had stayed there looking at him, calling to him, talking to him. And then she fell asleep on the threshold. Then he forgot all the horror of his "happy" life, he went to get her at the other door, he threw her on the bed and joined her, and he talked and talked in Chinese while she went on sleeping, and in the end he fell asleep, too.

The river. Far away. The way it curves through the rice paddies. It takes the place of the lovers.

126

Over the river, relative night. The white sky at day's dawning.

They are asleep.

Once, in her sleep that night, she called her little brother's name. The Chinese heard her say it. When she woke up, he told her. She didn't answer. She went back to the door. She fell asleep again.

They are asleep. Again she calls her abandoned little brother.

The Chinese wakes up.

Sitting by the other door, leaning up against it, she is watching him. She is naked. She can't make him out. She looks at him with all her strength. She says:

"It's almost daylight. I'm going to go to Sadec in your car to see my mother. I miss Paulo."

He hasn't heard her. She says again:

"I agree with your father. I don't want to stay with you. I want to leave, go back to my little brother."

He has heard her. He answers from the depths of sleep.

"You can say whatever you want, I don't care." He adds: "There's no point lying."

He doesn't move. She stays away from him. He is awake.

They look at each other. She leaves the door, she goes over to the fountain. She gets up, she goes to lie down under the shower in the basin.

She talks to him, she tells him she will always love him. She thinks she will love him all her life. It will be the same for him, too. They have both ruined themselves forever.

He doesn't answer. As though he hadn't heard.

So she sings in Vietnamese. And at that, he laughs. He laughs; then she laughs, too.

He has taken out his old opium kit. He has gone back to bed. He is smoking. He is calm. She is still lying down, her eyes closed now, stretched out in the basin. He's the one who talks about their affair for the first time.

He says:

"It's true, it was on the ferry that I thought that about you. I told myself you would never stay with any man."

"Never—not a single one?"

"Never."

Silence.

"Why did you think that?"

"Because as soon as you looked at me I wanted you."

She has her eyes shut. He doesn't know if she is really sleeping. He looks at her. No, she isn't sleeping: she has opened her eyes. He is smoking opium in front of her, this is the first time.

She says so:

"It's the first time you've smoked in front of me."

"It's when I'm unhappy. With opium, I can tolerate anything. Everyone smokes here, even the rickshaw boys."

"Women, too, I know that."

"In wealthy circles, yes. My mother smoked. We know how to smoke, it's a part of our culture. The whites don't know anything about it. The way they smoke opium, it makes us laugh to see them. And afterwards, the stupor they're in—"

He laughs.
Silence.
They both laugh.

The child looks at him. She rediscovers "the stranger on the ferry."

"Doing nothing is like a profession for you, having women, smoking opium. Going to clubs, the pool, Paris, New York, Florida . . ."

"Doing nothing is a profession. It's very hard."

"Maybe the hardest thing there is . . ."

"Maybe."

She comes over to him. He strokes her hair, looks at her, he discovers her again. He asks:

"You didn't know your father."

"I have two images of him. One in Hanoi, one at Phnom Penh. Otherwise no. The day he died, yes, I remember. My mother crying, screaming. Tell me again: to be rich, to do nothing and bear it, you need money and what else . . ."

"To be Chinese"—he smiles—"and play cards. I play a lot. When my chauffeur says I've gone out, that means I'm playing cards, often with the scum along the channels at night. Without gambling, you can't go on."

She has come back over to him. She is in the wicker chair by the basin.

"The first day I thought you were . . . not a moneybags, no, but wealthy, and a man who made love a lot and was afraid. Of what, I didn't know. I still don't know. I don't know how to say it, really—afraid of death, and at the same time of life, of living a life that someday must die, and always knowing it. Maybe afraid of not loving, too, of never forgetting—I don't know how to say this . . ."

"You don't want to say it."

"You're right, I don't want to."

Silence.

"No one knows how to say it."

"You're right."

"According to you, I'm frightened but I don't know it?"

Silence. The child reflects.

"No. You just don't know how frightened you are . . ."

Silence. She looks at him as though she had just met him. She says:

"I want to remember all of you, forever." She adds: "You who know nothing about yourself—when you were little, you were ill and you don't even know it . . ."

She looks at him, she takes his face in her hands, looks at him, she closes his eyes and looks some more.

He says:

"I see your eyes through my eyelids . . .

"I know a little of what you're saying about me. But how do you know it?"

"Because of my little brother. You can see a long, slightly curved track on his back, just like on yours. It's in the outline of the spinal column, under the skin."

"My mother said it was rickets. She took me to see a famous doctor in Tokyo."

She goes over to him, bends down, kisses his hand.

"I wish you didn't love me."

"I don't love you." (Pause.) "Is that what you want?"

She smiles, she trembles all of a sudden, she plays the game, she asks:

"It could be something you're just making up, for now . . ."

"Maybe."

"It's terrible to hear the words, to know the voice that is saying those words . . ."

He takes her in his arms, kisses her over and over.

He says:

"And that's what you want."

"Yes."

The Chinese says:

"Guess some more why I'm scared."

"Maybe something you're just making up—like loving me."

"Maybe. Because otherwise, if everything is given, you might just as well be dead?"

She doesn't answer. He goes on.

"You're saying that to live like me is like being dead?"

She cries out softly:

"What a stupid conversation to be having."

Silence. He presses her:

"There's just one more question I'd like to ask you."

She doesn't want him to. She says she doesn't know how to answer people. She asks:

"Besides me you've never slept with a white woman?"

"In Paris, of course. But not here."

"Can't you get white women here?"

"It's impossible. Though there are French prostitutes."

"They're expensive?"

"Very expensive."

"How much?"

The Chinese gives her a look. She laughs hard at that. Suddenly he lies. He says:

"I don't remember—a thousand piastres?"

He laughs with her.

"Just once I'd like you to say to me: 'I came to your place so that you would give me money.'"

A pause. She tries to think why. She can't lie. She can't say it. She says:

"No. That, that was afterwards. On the ferry, it wasn't the money. No. It was like it didn't exist."

He "sees" the ferry again. He says:

"Say it as though it did."

She says it the way he wants:

"On the ferry I saw you covered in gold, in a black car made of gold, with shoes made of gold. I think that's why I wanted you so badly, right away, on the ferry—but it wasn't just for that, I'm sure of it. Or maybe it was the gold I wanted, all the same, without knowing it."

The Chinese laughs. He says:

"The gold, that was me . . ."

"I don't know. Don't pay any attention to what I'm saying. I'm not used to talking like this."

"I am paying attention, all the same. But not to what you're saying. To you, to the way you're talking."

She takes his hand, looks, kisses that hand. She says:

"For me, it was your hands"—she starts over—"that's what I thought. I saw them taking off my dress, baring me completely to you while you looked at me."

Silence. He knew it. He knows it. He looks away. He smiles. The game suddenly turns violent. He yells as though he were about to strike her:

"You want the ring?"

The child screams. She cries. She screams. She doesn't take the ring.

A long silence.

And so the Chinese knew she had wanted the ring to give to her mother as much as she wanted his hand on her body, that she must only have realized it now from his question to her about the ring. He says:

"Forget it."

"I've forgotten it. I would never want something like that, a diamond. You can never sell a diamond when you're poor. They'd look at us, they'd think we stole it."

"Who's 'they'?"

"The Chinese diamond merchants—and from other races, too. But especially the Chinese. My mother, she knew a young woman who was poor, a man had given her a diamond, she tried for two years to sell it, nothing doing. So she gave the diamond back to the man who had given it to her and he gave her some money, but very little. It was the same thing, the man thought the diamond she was giving him back wasn't the same one he had given her, that the new diamond was worthless and she had stolen it from another man. My mother told me never to accept a diamond, just money."

The Chinese takes her in his arms. He says:

"So you, you look like a poor person?"

Silence. She asks:

"Does a ring like that cost much?"

"Very much."

"Very, very much or very much."

"I don't know."

They look at the foreign ring. And then the Chinese says:

"It could be worth tens of thousands of piastres. All I know is, the diamond was my mother's. It was part of her dowry. My father had it set for me by a famous Paris jeweler after her death. The jeweler, he came to Manchuria to pick up the diamond. And he came back to Manchuria to deliver the ring."

She says:

"Do you believe that?"

He doesn't speak, he leaves her. He loves her. She laughs hard suddenly. She says:

"It's true, a diamond isn't something you'd send in a tiny little package by mail, is it . . ."

She laughs. She explodes with laughter. She says she can see the diamond, all by itself in a big armored truck. She says you can't transport a diamond; even when it's "enormous," it's too small—and she laughs—no bigger than a pea.

He is always happy when she laughs. Cheery, the way I was at her age, the mother would say.

He says:

"I know you didn't see the diamond right away."

"No, I did see it, but separate from you. I'm sure of that. Just the same, I knew what a diamond was. I smelled it, it smelled good, like you—incense, tussore, cologne. I didn't think of it for me, for me to wear, I mean. I think people are born poor. Even if someday I'm rich, I'll be stuck with a poor woman's bad attitude, a poor woman's body and face, my whole life I'll look that way.

Like my mother. She looks poor, though with her you don't totally believe it."

He disagrees. To him, she looks like a peasant—she is beautiful the way a peasant woman is beautiful.

She gives him another very straight look. She says:

"But you, you look rich. And your fiancée, what does she look like?"

"Nothing special. Like a rich woman. Like me."

The child takes the hand that wears the diamond. She looks at the ring, the diamond. She lowers her eyes. He is looking at her. He says:

"Repeat what you said to me earlier."

She repeats:

"I wanted you right away, very quickly, very much at that moment. It's true."

"As much as your little brother?"

She thinks it over. She says:

"I don't know how to say it: my little brother, he's also my child . . ."

"Your little brother has never had you."

"No. I've done it to him, with my hands."

They remain entwined. He says very low that he, too, loves the little brother.

They light incense sticks. They sing. They talk. The child strokes her lover's body. She says:

"You have a rain skin too."

"Your little brother too."

"Yes, him too, all three of us have a rain skin."

The nights become exhausting. It keeps getting hotter. People go to the banks of the waterways to sleep. In the distance, you can see the piers of the Messageries Maritimes. They go there too. Sometimes it's the Chinese who drives. This frightens the chauffeur and the child.

The Chinese holds the child to him, always, everywhere. He says:

"I love you like my child, too, the same."

The bachelor quarters.

The child informs the Chinese that the repatriation the mother had requested for the older brother has finally been confirmed.

"For when?"

"Soon. I don't know anything more definite."

"I knew through my father that your brother was on the list of upcoming departures."

"He knows everything, your father."

"Yes. He knows everything that concerns you, too."

"Everything, really?"

"Yes."

"How does he do it?"

"He pays. He buys. Even when he doesn't owe them any-thing, he pulls out the piastres—it's very funny."

"If you think about it, it's disgusting . . ."

"I suppose so. I don't care. He pulls out the piastres when there's absolutely no need. It's in his blood."

She is crying. He takes her face in his hands. She trembles. She says:

"I slept with you so you would give me money, even if I didn't know it."

He pulls her even closer to him. That fear of him has grown even greater. He says:

"I have something to tell you. It's a little difficult to say this: I'm going to give you money for your mother. From my father. She knows about it."

The child seems not to have heard. Then she violently pulls free—the child knows nothing about the visit the Chinese has made to her mother. She says:

"How can that be, my mother doesn't even know you exist."

Very abruptly, she has begun addressing him formally again. He doesn't answer.

Tears in her eyes, she suddenly doubts him. She looks at him as though he were a criminal. She says:

"You've been making inquiries about my family."

The Chinese stands up to the child. He says:

"Yes. I went to Sadec to see your mother, at my father's request. To talk to her. To learn about your family's poverty."

He is very pained and full of love for her. He says:

"It's true you have nothing left. The only thing they had left to sell was you. And no one wants to buy you. Your older brother had written to my father. Your mother wanted to meet me. My father asked me to see her. I saw her."

The child straightens up. She pulls even further away from him: he becomes the man who has seen her mother in misery, in the obscenity of misfortune. She says:

"How could you dare—"

The Chinese is cautious, very sweet:

"She's known everything since the beginning of our affair. At first she was horrified at the thought of her daughter marrying a Chinese. And then she hoped we would marry. We talked for a long time. What I wanted was, I wanted her to stop hoping we would marry. Under any circumstances. To rid herself of the idea forever. I reminded her of Chinese law. I talked to her about my father's preferring me dead to violating the law."

The child is crying. She says—using the familiar address again:

"I could have told her it was me, that I didn't want to marry you—ever, at any price—that I couldn't care less about getting married, about any of it. It would have been less humiliating for her."

"But she wasn't humiliated, I swear it. We even laughed together . . ."

"About what?"

"About Chinese law. And my father."

"She likes to laugh, my mother. She's kept that . . ."

"Yes. I told her I knew her son's departure date through my father. I asked her how much she needed for his departure. She told me 250 piastres."

The Chinese and the child laugh. Then the child cries and

smiles at the same time. And then the Chinese stops laughing, he looks at the child, he says:

"Your mother, she makes you want to love you, to love her child."

The child suddenly talks like a grown-up:

"You'll have to give her a lot. There are expenses on the boat, if you want to travel comfortably. The trip has been paid for, but that's not everything. Just for winter clothes, board, tuition at a technical school, the Violet curriculum . . ."

He goes over to the shower to get his jacket, he takes an envelope from a pocket, he says:

"How much does she need for right now? I've brought 500 piastres."

"Five hundred piastres for right now—sure, why not?"

He lays the envelope on the table.

She undresses. She takes off her dress in a single motion, pulling from the top. He still can't see that gesture without feeling something. He says:

"What are you doing?"

She says she is going to take another shower. She adds that, at last, she is satisfied for her mother. She says she will give the envelope to Thanh, so he can hide it, and only he will know where. She says she can't give it directly to her mother, because her older brother would steal all the money within hours. And her mother would be unhappy.

The Chinese says:

"Her son would steal it, or she would give it to her son?"

"Yes, well, it's all the same."

"Thanh will guard the money—you swear it?"

"I swear it."

The child has taken her shower. She gets dressed again.
She says she is going back to the boarding school.
"Why?"
"I want to be by myself."
"No. You're staying with me. We'll go to the bars along the
waterways, we'll drink choum, we'll eat nem-nuongs. That's
where they're the best, the women make them themselves, and
the choum comes from the countryside."
"Can I go back to the boarding school afterward?"
"No."
She laughs. She says:
"I'll go back anyway. Afterward."
He laughs with her. No one can resist the little bars along
the waterways, the choum and the nems from the countryside.
Or the port either, at night.

They head toward the docks at the Messageries. He has
pulled her against him on the seat. He tries to kiss her. She
resists, then lets herself be kissed.
He is in the middle of it, loving this cruel, unpredictable,
skinny, nearly flat-chested child.
They stop by an ocean liner that is about to sail.
There is an open dance floor on the ship's forward deck.
White women are dancing with the officers. They aren't
wearing makeup. They look docile, like forced labor.
The dancers do not speak to one another—as though it
were forbidden by law. The women are particularly serious:

140

dancing is their profession, they smile like nuns, at peace with the world, on principle. They are wearing light, discreetly flowered dresses. The child observes these things with a sort of fascination. When they reach the other side of the port, she detaches herself from the Chinese and watches the bloodless dancing on the deck.

The Chinese resists this detour in their excursion. But he always winds up going where the child wants to go.

For a long time, the child never understood why she was fascinated, much as the Chinese hadn't understood. And then one day she remembered: she recovered the image of those couples bloodlessly, wordlessly dancing on deck, recovered it intact and as though it were already integrated into a book she hadn't taken on yet but must have been on the verge of tackling every morning, every day of her life for years and years, and which demanded to be written—until she reached that moment of clear memory in the forest of writing still to come.*

They cross the whole breadth of the insomniac city, beaten down by the heat of the night. There isn't a breath of air.

She is asleep. The Chinese listens to the chauffeur singing a song from Manchuria, wild and sweet, howling and murmured.

He carries her over to the bed.

He puts out the light.

He smokes opium in the twilight of the room.

Some music reaches them as it does every night, Chinese

---

*It became *Emily L.*

141

songs, far away. And then, late in the night, very low, Duke Ellington's trains come along, down the street and through the doors to the rooms. And then, even later and lower and more alone, that desperation waltz from when their love affair began.

EDEN CINEMA/SAIGON

The chauffeur, outside the school.

He waits until the doors close.

The child doesn't come.

He leaves. He drives down rue Catinat.

He see the child with a young white man who must be her brother and a very handsome, similarly dressed young native man. The three of them are coming out of the Eden Cinema.

The chauffeur goes back to Cholon to let his master know.

The Chinese is waiting in the bachelor quarters.

The chauffeur tells him about the Eden Cinema.

The Chinese says the child goes to the movies often, she has told him so, the two young men with her are Thanh, her mother's chauffeur, and her younger brother, Paulo.

They go to join them.

The child comes out of the movie theater with Thanh and her little brother. She goes straight over to the black car, she is very natural. She smiles at the Chinese, she says:

"My family is here from Vinh-Long. I went to the movies with Thanh and Paulo. I told them you had invited them to dinner at the restaurant in Cholon."

She laughs. He starts laughing too. The fear vanishes. The little brother and Thanh say hello to the Chinese. The little brother seems not to recognize the Chinese, but he says hello, too. He looks at him, this Chinese, the way a child would, he doesn't understand why the Chinese is looking at him so hard. He forgets he's seen him before on the streets of Sadec. Thanh, by contrast, recognizes him.

The child says she thinks she didn't like the film, *The Blue Angel,* but she can't say for sure, she can't really tell yet.

She also says her mother and older brother have just arrived in the B-12.*

The older brother doesn't say hello to the Chinese. The mother does, she smiles at him: Good day, Monsieur. How are things?

The Chinese is moved to see this woman again, beside her daughter.

The little brother, the older brother, and the mother get into the B-12.

The Chinese says with a smile:

"When they're here, you don't love me."

She takes his hand, kisses it. She says:

"I don't know. I wanted you to see them just once in your

---

*The B-12 isn't the "wreck" it becomes in *The Sea Wall.* At this point it's in rough shape, of course, but it doesn't backfire, it doesn't smoke up the streets of the posts in-country, it isn't an oddity.

life. Yes, maybe it's true that their being here keeps me from seeing you, you yourself."

The Chinese restaurant.

This is the restaurant where the child and the Chinese went on the first evening of their affair. It's the part of the restaurant without music. The noise from the main room is not overpowering.

The waiter comes over, he asks if they would like a drink.

They place their order. Three Martel Perriers and one bottle of rice wine.

They have nothing to say to one another. No one speaks. Stillness. No one is surprised by it, bothered by it.

The drinks arrive. A general stillness. No one minds, neither they nor the child. That's how it is.

In fact, they suddenly seem delighted with life, with playing at living.

The older brother orders a second Martel Perrier. The mother hasn't touched hers, she gives it to her older son. The mother's behavior surprises no one.

They order food all around. Glazed duck. Chinese shark-fin soup, prawn-flavored crêpes. The family orders only the "specialties of the house." The most expensive dishes, of course.

The mother reads the menu, she cries out softly: "Oh my, look how expensive." No one responds.

144

And then the mother, polite, proper, makes an attempt to talk with the Chinese:

"I understand you've studied in Paris, Monsieur."

The mother and the Chinese smile ironically at each other. They seem almost well-acquainted. The Chinese takes up the mother's tone in his answer:

"Well, not really, Madame . . ."

"Sort of like us, then," says the older brother.

Silence.

The older brother laughs. Paulo and Thanh laugh, too.

The Chinese, to the older brother:

"So you don't do anything for a living, either?"

"Oh, but I do: I'm ruining my family, that's something."

The Chinese laughs freely. Everyone laughs, the mother too, delighted to have such a "witty" son. And Paulo and Thanh too.

The Chinese asks:

"A tough thing to do?"

"Let's just say not everyone has the gift."

The Chinese pushes him:

"What does it take most of all?"

"Nastiness. Nastiness of the first water, you understand, like a diamond."

No one laughs except the Chinese and the mother.

The child looks at those two, her mother and her lover, the new arrivals in her own, the child's story.

The older brother says out loud to the mother:

"He all right, this guy, he can take care of himself."

The food arrives, everyone helps himself. The Chinese offers to serve the mother.

They eat in silence. They "exaggerate" their eating. All four of them eat "alike," even the child.

The Chinese sees the child gaze on them, her family, a loving, joyous gaze at these people who are finally out, out of the house in Sadec, off the post, finally loosed on the city, on display for all eyes, feasting busily on lichee nuts in syrup.

The mother smiles at life. She speaks. She says:

"It's nice to see them eat."

The mother talks—"just to talk," not to say anything. She's happy. Says whatever comes into her head. She and the child, both chatter the same way, nonstop. Nonstop chatterers, that's what they are. In ecstasy, the Chinese looks at her, her and the child, her and her resemblance to the child. The mother says:

"I like this restaurant, it's nice. We ought to get the address."

No one laughs. Not the Chinese. Nor Thanh. Nor the older brother.

The Chinese takes a pen, writes the address on a menu, which he gives the mother. The mother says:

"Thank you, Monsieur. You know, I think this is a very good restaurant, as good as the ones in-country that people consider the best in Indochina because they aren't at all 'inauthentic' in the French style."

They all stuff themselves. The Chinese, who wasn't eating, begins stuffing himself, too. He has ordered grilled prawns and devours them. So the others order more grilled prawns and they devour them, too. By the end, no one is making any effort to talk. They watch the waiters at their work with a passion, it interests them. They keep waiting for "what's next." With the help of the rice wine, they are at peace. They drink. The mother, too, she says she loves that stuff, the choum-choum. She is twenty years old. When the desserts come, the mother is dozing off. The children eat the desserts, they're still exaggerating. This time the older brother has a whiskey, the others don't. The Chinese drinks more than the little brother. The girl drinks from the Chinese's glass. The mother no longer really knows what she's drinking, she laughs to herself, happy this evening the way other people are.

At the center of this world, the Chinese is watching the child enter on a happiness he hasn't given her—he, her lover.

Suddenly the older brother gets up. He's talking like the boss. He speaks to all of them. He says:

"Well, it isn't over. What happens now?"

The mother wakes with a start. Which makes everyone around the table laugh one last time, even Thanh. She asks what's happening.

Laughing, the older brother says they're all going to the Cascade. Come on, let's go—

Laughing like her son, the mother says:

"So, we're celebrating. It's true—as long as we're at it, why not enjoy ourselves."

The child, the Chinese, and Thanh and Paulo—everyone is happy. They're all going to the Cascade.

Discreetly, speaking a "very pure" Chinese, the Chinese has asked for the check. They bring it on a saucer. The Chinese takes out a roll of ten-piastre notes and piles eight of them on the saucer. Silence falls at the sum. The mother and the older brother look at each other. Everyone calculates in his head how much the Chinese must have paid, subtracting the change left

147

over on the saucer. The child knows what's going on and she starts laughing again. The mother is nearly in hysterics over the enormity of the sum. A small cry escapes her: "Seventy-seven piastres!" and she chokes with laughter, "Oh dear," and goes off in a child's fit of irrepressible giggles.

They leave the restaurant. They walk to the cars.

The child and the Chinese laugh.

The Chinese says to the child:

"They're children—even your older brother."

"They're the most important children in my life. The funniest, too, for me. The craziest. The most awful. But also, the ones who make me laugh the most. My older brother, sometimes I forget about him, I can't quite believe he is what he is, except when I'm afraid he's going to kill Paulo. When he's at the opium den all night, I think I'd be perfectly happy if he died; I'd be perfectly happy even if he died of it during the day."

The child asks whether things are different when there is a father in the family.

The Chinese says it's just the same. He says:

"Even in families with a father, even when the father is as powerful, as terrible as can be, he still gets dragged into his children's nastiness and bickering."

Suddenly the child is fighting off tears. She says she had forgotten this was the last time Pierre would see Saigon, maybe for the rest of his life.

It is the Chinese who tells her the date, time, and dock number of her brother's departure.

The child says the older brother's brutality toward Paulo was more and more frequent, and for no reason. He would say: As soon as I see him I want to kill him. He couldn't resist hitting

148

him, insulting him. Thanh had told the mother that if Pierre didn't leave for France, the little brother would die of despair, or his brother Pierre would kill him. Even he, Thanh, was afraid, and for the mother's sake, too. The Chinese asks: And for the little sister's? She says: For me, no.

Once, the Chinese had asked Thanh what he thought about that. Thanh said: No, not her, she isn't in any danger.

The child comes close to the Chinese. She puts her hand over her face to say it:

"The reason we still love him is because he doesn't realize he's a born criminal. He'll never understand that, even if he kills Paulo someday."

They talk about Paulo. He thinks he is very handsome, Thanh too; he says you'd think they were brothers, Thanh and Paulo.

She isn't listening. She says:

"After the Cascade, we'll go get the money. I'll go back with them to the Hotel Charner. Whenever my mother comes to Saigon, I stay there with her, like when I was small. We talk . . ."

"About what?"

"About life"—she smiles—"about her dying"—she smiles—"like you with your mother in Manchuria, after the girl from Canton."

"She must know a lot, your mother."

No, the child says, no, with her it's the other way around, by now she doesn't know anything anymore. She knows everything—and nothing. It's somewhere between the two that she still knows things, but none of us can say what. She may still know the names of villages in the north of France, like Fruges, Bonnières, Doulens, and cities too, Dunkerque, where she had her first teaching position and got married the first time, to an inspector in the primary schools.

The Cascade is situated over a stream fed by springs, on untended grounds on the outskirts of Saigon. All of them are on the dance floor, in the coolness of the springs. There's no one there yet except two half-castes behind the bar, hostesses waiting for customers. As soon as customers come in, they put on records. A young Vietnamese waiter comes to take their order. All the staff are in white.

The Chinese and the girl dance together.

The older brother watches them. He snickers, he makes fun of them.

The curse returns. It is there in his obscene, forced laughter.

The Chinese asks the child:

"What is he laughing at?"

"My dancing with you."

The child and the Chinese start laughing themselves. And then everything changes. The older brother's laugh becomes a false, cutting laugh. He says, he shouts it:

"Pardon me, it's my nerves. I can't help myself—you're so ill-matched—I can't help laughing."

The Chinese lets go of the child. He crosses the dance

floor. He heads toward the older brother, seated at the table beside the mother. He comes very close to him. He looks at him feature by feature, as though he were passionately interested.

The older brother gets scared.

Then the Chinese says very calmly, softly, with a smile:

"Excuse me, I don't know you very well, but you intrigue me. Why are you making yourself laugh. What are you hoping . . ."

The older brother is scared:

"I'm not after anything, but I'm always ready for a fight."

The Chinese laughs good-naturedly:

"I've studied kung fu. I always warn people beforehand."

The mother gets scared, too. She cries out:

"Don't mind him, he's been drinking . . ."

The older brother is more and more afraid.

"What is this—can't I laugh?"

The Chinese laughs:

"No."

"What don't you like about my laugh? Say it."

The Chinese looks for the word. He can't find it, that word.

That's what he says, the word for it may not exist. Then he finds it:

"False, it's false. That's the word: false. You're the only one who thinks you're laughing. But you aren't."

The little brother gets up, he goes over to the bar, he asks one of the half-castes to dance. He doesn't listen to the Chinese talking with Pierre.

The older brother remains standing by his chair, not going toward the Chinese. He sits down again and says under his breath:

"Who does that guy think he is . . ."

The Chinese continues dancing with the child.

They dance.

The number ends.

The older brother goes to the bar. He orders a Martel Perrier.

The older brother sits far from the Chinese. The Chinese sits down beside the mother, who is still frightened. Trembling, she asks him:

"Have you really studied Chinese combat, Monsieur?"

The Chinese laughs. He says:

"Oh, no, hardly—never, Madame, never. You can't imagine how little I've studied that; it's the other way around, Madame . . ."

The mother smiles and says:

"Thank you, Monsieur, thank you."

She adds:

"Is it true that in China all the rich study it?"

The Chinese doesn't know. He isn't listening to the mother anymore. Fascinated, he is watching the older brother. He says:

"It's strange how your son makes you want to hit him. Forgive me . . ."

The mother comes closer to the Chinese, says privately that she knows it, it's really a terrible thing. She adds:

"My daughter must have told you. Forgive him, Monsieur—forgive me most of all, I've brought my children up badly, I'm the one who most deserves the punishment."

The mother. She looks at him over by the bar, she says she's going to take him back to the hotel, he's drunk.

The Chinese smiles. He says:

"I'm the one who should apologize, Madame. I shouldn't have answered him back; suddenly I couldn't help it, though. Don't leave because of that . . ."

"Thank you, Monsieur. I know what you're saying, though—he does give you the urge to hit him, that child."

"He's a mean one, is that it?"

The mother hesitates. And then she says:

"Yes, perhaps, but cruel more, you understand. That's it, really, that awful thing—cruelty, the pleasure he takes in doing evil; it's so mysterious, and also the way he knows how to do it, the genius he has for it, for evil."

The mother becomes reflective. She says:

"In French, we call it the devil's cunning."

The Chinese says:

"In China we say: the cunning of demons, of evil spirits."

"It's all comes back to the same thing, Monsieur."

"I agree, Madame."

Then the Chinese looks at the mother for a long time, and she becomes frightened. She asks what the problem is. The Chinese says:

"I would like you to tell me the truth, Madame, about your daughter. Has your son hit her . . ."

Frightened, the mother gives a low whimper. But the older brother hasn't heard. The mother hesitates, she gives the Chinese a long look. She answers:

"No, Monsieur, I did, because I was afraid he would kill her."

The Chinese smiles at the mother.

"On orders from him, from your older son?"

"You could say that, but it isn't that simple. Out of love for him, to make him happy . . . not to put him in the wrong for a change. You understand . . ."

The mother is crying. From far off, the son has noticed something. He moves toward them. He stops when the Chinese starts looking at him. The mother doesn't heed him. Softly she asks the Chinese if "her girl" has talked to him about it.

The Chinese says no, never, that he had figured it out that evening, that he had suspected it before because of the sort of childish fear that never left the child—a sort of constant fear, distrust of everything, storms, darkness, beggars, the sea, Chinese—he smiles at the mother—of himself, of everything.

The mother is crying very softly. The Chinese has started watching the son with conspicuous detachment, he looks at his handsome face, his careful grooming, his elegance. Without taking his eyes off him, he asks the mother what word the son used. She says it was the phrase "break her"—like training an animal—but mostly it was the word "lost"—that if they didn't do something, she and he, the girl would be lost; he was sure of it, she would "go with" any man.

"You believed it, Madame?"

"I still believe it, Monsieur."

She looks at him.

"And you, Monsieur?"

"I've thought so since the first day, Madame. As soon as I saw her on the ferry and began to love her."

They smile at each other through their tears. The Chinese says:

154

"Even if she was 'lost,' I would have loved her my whole life."

He also asks:

"How long did the beatings last?"

"Until the day Paulo saw the three of us, my son and me shut up in the room with my girl. He couldn't bear it. He threw himself at him."

The mother adds:

"It was the most frightening moment of my life."

The Chinese asks in a whisper, holding his breath:

"Which of your sons were you afraid for, Madame?"

The mother looks at the Chinese, she gets up to leave, then sits down again.

The Chinese says:

"Forgive me."

The mother takes hold of herself, she says:

"You ought to know, Monsieur, that it is sacred even to love a dog. And we have the right—as sacred as life itself—not to have to justify it to anyone."

The Chinese lowers his eyes and he cries. He says he will never forget that: ". . . even a dog . . ."

The child is dancing with Thanh. She talks to him in a low voice:

"Later, I'm going to give you 500 piastres for Mother. You won't give them to her. You will hide them first, and watch out for Pierre when you do it."

Thanh says he knows where and how.

155

"Even if he kills me, I won't tell about the 500 piastres. Since he's smoking all the time, me, I'm stronger than him."

As they dance, Thanh inhales the child's hair, he kisses her like when they are alone. No one pays it any mind, neither the family nor the Chinese. The Chinese watches the child dancing with Thanh, all jealousy banished. He has returned to the infinite space of his separation from the child—lost, inconsolable. The mother sees his pain. She says to him, all charm:

"My daughter makes you suffer a great deal, Monsieur."

The older son has remained where he was, by the dance floor. He sees the danger is receding, that the Chinese is amusing himself, and he says out loud:

"Filthy chink."

The Chinese smiles at the mother.

"Yes, Madame, she makes me suffer more than I have the strength to."

Drunk, charming, the mother cries over the Chinese.

"Monsieur, I believe you, it must be terrible. And how kind of you to talk to me about my child with such openness. We could talk for nights on end, you and I, don't you think?"

"Yes, Madame, it's true. We would talk about her and about you." (Pause.) "So your son said that it was for her own good he was beating her—and in your opinion he believed this?"

"Yes, Monsieur. I know it's strange, but it's true. And I can swear to it."

The Chinese takes the mother's hand, he kisses it. He says:

156

"It's also possible he saw she was in danger . . ."
The mother is amazed and she cries. She says:
"Life is terrible, Monsieur. If you only knew . . ."

The child and Thanh have stopped dancing. The child says:
"In the envelope there is a second, separate package with
200 piastres, which is for you."
Thanh is surprised:
"From him?"
"From him, yes. Don't try to understand."
Thanh is silent. And then he says:
"I will keep. For me later on—return to Siam."

The Chinese has gone to a table to sit down. Probably to be
alone. He is alone in the city, and in life as well—with the love
in his heart for this child who is going away, leaving him, his
body, forever. A terrible mourning inhabits the Chinese. And
the white child knows it.

She looks at him, and for the first time she realizes that the
solitude has always been there, between her and him, a Chinese solitude that protected him, was like his country around
him. Even as it was the place for their bodies, their love.

Already the child sensed that this affair might be one about
love.

The little brother dances with the young half-caste from
the bar. Thanh, too, watches Paulo dancing with miraculous

grace. Paulo has never studied dancing. The child says this to Thanh, who didn't know it yet.

Only the mother and the older brother stand outside the group focus of this scene. Each of them, alone, watches Paulo dance.*

The little brother comes back from dancing. He asks his sister to dance. They have always danced together, it's marvellous to see: the little brother dances as though in his sleep, apparently without even realizing he is dancing. He doesn't look at his sister and his sister doesn't look at him, either. They dance together without knowing how to dance. They will never in their lives dance like this again. Princes when they dance, those two, says the mother. Sometimes they laugh their own private laugh, malicious, inimitable, no one can figure out why. They don't say a word, just looking at each other makes them laugh. And around them, people rejoice at the sight. As for them, they don't know it.

The Chinese cries to see them. Under his breath, he says the word: worship.

The mother hears him. She says yes, that's it, that's the word for what's between those two children.

---

*In the film, all the action would occur this way, through the gaze. The gaze would be the continuity. Those who watch are watched, in turn, by others. The camera bars exchange: it only films people, which is to say the solitude of the individual (here, everyone takes his turn dancing). There's no point taking long shots here, because the group doesn't exist here. These are isolated individuals, random "solitudes." Passion is the continuity of the film.

We hear the older brother's voice. He is speaking to his mother.

"Paulo ought to avoid making a fool of himself like that in public, he dances like a clod. This has to stop. He'll just have to learn . . ."

No one seems to have heard him except for her, the child, and even that isn't certain.

The little brother and his sister have finished dancing. She goes over to the Chinese, alone at his table. She wants to dance with him. They dance.

She says:

"I was worried earlier."

"That I might kill him."

"Yes."

The child starts smiling at the Chinese again. She says:

"You can't possibly understand."

"I understand a little."

"Maybe you're right, that I won't ever love you. I'm saying that for right now. I'm not saying anything else. For now, for this evening, I don't love you, and I never will love you."

The Chinese doesn't answer.

The child goes on.

"I would have preferred for you not to love me. For you to do what you usually do, like you do with other women. That's what I wanted. You didn't have to go and love me too."

Silence.

"We're all leaving, even Paulo. Except Thanh. You will be alone with your wife in the blue house."

He says he knows that as deeply as you can know anything.

They go on dancing.

The moment is drawn out.

They stop dancing.

"I want you to dance with one of the girls from the dance hall. For me to see you once with another woman."

The Chinese hesitates. Then he goes and asks the prettiest of the hostesses, the one who danced with Paulo.

It's a tango.

The child faces them, leans against the railing that circles the dance hall: that man from the ferry in light tussore silk, his supple, summery elegance, overdone here, misplaced. Degraded.

She watches.

He is lost in pain. The pain of knowing he doesn't have the strength to steal her away from the law. Of knowing there's no way around it, that he knows as well, just as he knows he will never kill his father, never rob him, never carry the child away by boat, by train to hide with her, far, very far away. If he knows the law, he also knows himself before the law.

The Chinese comes back from dancing.

The child talks about money, about the horror of not being able to do without it, not being able either to stay or to go. She says:

"What it is, is the debts. It's true that you, you can't understand that. It drives us crazy. My mother's salary mostly goes for that, for paying the interest on the debts. That's the biggest

160

expense. Paying for dead, unworkable, stolen rice paddies you can't even give away to the poor."

The Chinese says:

"I want to talk to you about your brother Pierre. Last week, I saw him in front of the opium den by the river. He asked me for a hundred piastres. I gave it to him. I think he's going to go on drugging himself until he dies, and he'll do awful things along the way. He'll do anything, the worst."

The Chinese says further:

"The worst will be in France when he's without opium. Then he will take cocaine, and then he will be very dangerous. Your mother must get Paulo away from him, and quickly. You, too, he may prostitute you, and he'll do it without hesitating, to buy drugs. He's still scared of you, but not for much longer. To me, it's as if you were living with a murderer."

The child tells him:

"He has already tried prostituting me. It was a doctor from Saigon who was passing through Sadec. Thanh heard it from the doctor himself. Thanh wanted to kill him."

The child stops dancing. She asks the Chinese:

"A hundred piastres, you would have given that to anyone . . ."

"Yes."

The child laughs. She says:

"Why?"

"I don't really know. Maybe so he would be more bearable for your mother. No. It's because I like opium. That's it, that's all. I understand him."

"We've all thought of killing him, even my mother. A hundred piastres, that's what I was worth to him. That was also how much he asked from the doctor who was passing through . . ."

Silence. He smiles. He asks:

"You didn't like him?"

"No. Before you, it was Thanh I liked."

The Chinese knew it.

He says he's leaving, he's going to play cards in Cholon. The chauffeur will come back to the Cascade to get her and take her to the bachelor quarters to get the money. She says:

"I'm going to give Thanh the money this evening. He will give it to my mother in Sadec."

The number ends. The Chinese goes to say goodbye to the mother. He forgets to pay, then remembers: he goes over and puts a hundred piastres on the saucer left for that purpose at what had been their table. The waiter takes the money, goes to make change, comes back, puts the change on the saucer. The Chinese has left, he has forgotten his change.

Then, slowly, the older brother gets up and goes to the bar. Then he comes back to the saucer, lets his hand trail across the table.

Only the child and Thanh see as the older brother takes the money. They laugh. They don't talk about it. They laugh. Sometimes the child and Thanh laugh to see the older brother stealing money. It's done: he has put it in his pocket.

That evening, he was frightened by the waiter who had gone to the table to collect his tip and who yelled at the customers who were *forgetting the tip*. As soon as the older brother saw him, he went out to wait for the others in the B-12,

162

declaring that for his part he was leaving. The child had forgotten: the older brother gets scared. She is frightened again. Thanh is frightened for the older brother, too.

The younger brother goes on dancing as though nothing had happened, he hasn't noticed the scene.

The older brother comes back and shouts:

"Come on, come on, let's get out of this miserable place."

He panics, orders the little brother to leave immediately. The child places herself between the two brothers. She says he's waiting until the number is over.

The older brother waits.

The mother is drunk. She laughs at everything—the theft of the money by her son, her son's fear, his panic—as though it were a very animated, sporty, very comic comedy, one she knows by heart and always enjoys, the way she might a child's lack of common sense.

The older brother goes back out into the courtyard of the Cascade.

Someone from the Cascade comes to tell them the dance hall is closing. The music stops. The bar closes.

The child says to Thanh:

"We really are a family of scum."

Thanh says it doesn't matter. He laughs.

The child tells Thanh she is going with him to get the money at the bachelor quarters, that he will find her in rue Lyautey by the ditches where Alice prostitutes herself. He knows where that is. He remembers the story the child told him about Alice and the strangers who stopped their cars where she is telling him to.

The child talked with Thanh about everything except her

affair with the Chinese from Sadec. And she, she never talked about Thanh except with the Chinese from Sadec.

Everyone left the dance hall.

The limousine is lit up inside like a prison.

It is empty. The chauffeur is waiting for the child.

The older brother has fallen asleep in the B-12.

The whole family looks and doesn't understand where the Chinese has gone. Except for Thanh and the child, who are in hysterics.

The mother and her older son climb into the back seat of the B-12.

The little brother sits next to Thanh, as usual.

The chauffeur opens the door to the Léon Bollée.

The child climbs in back.

The family watches, stunned. They are still waiting for the Chinese, then give up trying to make sense of it when they see the little sister take off all by herself in the Léon Bollée.

She laughs. The chauffeur too.

The chauffeur says in French:

"My master said, we go to Cholon."

The chauffeur pulls up in front of the bachelor quarters. He opens the door. The girl gets out, goes quietly into the bachelor quarters. She acts as though someone were sleeping, she closes the door the same way. She looks: there's no one there. This is a first. She takes her time.

There is a large, unsealed envelope on the table.

She doesn't take it right away. She sits down in the armchair by the table. She stays like that, shut in with the money.

Outside, the chauffeur has turned off the Léon Bollée's engine.

The silence is almost total, except for the dogs who are always barking in the distance along the channels. In the big envelope, there are two others, the one for the mother and the one for Thanh. The stacks of bills are still in their bank wrappers. The child doesn't take them out of the envelopes, she pushes them back instead to the bottom of the big yellow envelope that holds everything.

She goes on sitting there. The lover's black dressing gown is on the armchair, funereal, scary. The place has already been vacated forever. She cries. Still sitting. She is alone with the money, she is moved at being there with the money she has managed to bring in. This is what she has done together with her mother: they have gotten—the money. Slowly, quietly, she cries. From insight. Unspeakable sadness. No pain, no, there's none of that. She takes her bookbag. She puts the envelope in the bookbag. She gets up. She turns off the light. She goes out.

We stay there, where she was.

It goes dark in the bachelor quarters.

We hear the key in the lock. Then the Léon Bollée's engine. Then its fading in the distance, its mingling with the city.

Lyautey Boarding School.

The courtyard is empty.

The young houseboys are singing and playing cards over by the refectory, as they do every evening.

The child takes off her shoes, goes up to the dormitory. The windows are open facing the street behind the boarding school.

A few girls are at the windows, watching Alice prostitute herself in the ditch along the unlit street. Two counselors are watching along with the boarders. It is one of the last streets in Saigon, the one with the boarding school for half-caste girls who have been abandoned by their white fathers.*

The child goes over and looks into the street. A man moving on top of a woman. The man and the women are dressed in white.

The prostitution has taken place. Alice and her lover get up again.

Hélène Lagonelle is among the girls watching.

The child goes to bed. Hélène Lagonelle and the other girls also go to bed.

Alice comes in. She crosses the dormitory, she puts out the light, she gets into bed.

The child gets up. She crosses the hall, the courtyard, goes out. She goes into the street where she will meet with Thanh.

Very softly, singing it, she calls Thanh's name.

---

*On the vast rice paddy of Camau, where the wetlands of Cochin China end, white functionaries were required at the time to leave their wives behind, because malaria and plague were endemic on the Plain of Birds, recently risen from the sea.

The child and Thanh.

Thanh comes out of the shadows behind the boarding school. She goes to him. They embrace. Without a word. She says she has the money.

They fetch the B-12 from behind the boarding school. She gets in back, lies down. They look at each other. He knows.

He doesn't say anything, he drives to the zoo. There's no one there. He stops the car near the fence, behind the large cat pavilion. She says:

"I used to come here all by myself on Thursdays. And then later I came with you."

They look at each other. Thanh says:

"You are his mistress."

"Yes. You were hoping not."

"Yes."

The little chauffeur moans. He talks in Vietnamese. He doesn't look at her anymore. She says:

"Come, Thanh."

"No."

"You and I, we've always wanted it. Come. There's no reason to be afraid anymore. Come to me, Thanh."

"No. I can't. You are my sister."

He comes. They kiss, inhale one another. Cry. Fall asleep without making love.

The child wakes up. It is still the middle of the night. She calls to Thanh, she tells him they have to be at the Hotel Charner before daybreak.

She falls back asleep.

Thanh looks at her sleeping for a long moment and then he heads toward the Hotel Charner.

Hotel Charner. The room.

The little brother is there. He is asleep.

Thanh separates the second bed. He lies down on the box spring.

In low voices, they talk about the mother. He has talked with the mother about Pierre. He tells the child:

"Last week, Pierre robbed the people at La Fumerie du Mékong again. She told me if he didn't pay them back he would go to jail. The idea of jail terrifies her. Even if he has to leave quickly for France, she must pay the den. It will stop when he leaves. She has to keep the money for that, too—to pay off the opium den. I don't know how she doesn't go crazy, our mother."

The child says:

"She is going crazy. You know it."

"Yes. I know."

The child adds:

"Yes. Don't say anything to our mother about the money. She'd let Pierre steal it the same night."

"I know all that. I'll go pay the opium den myself. Then I'll put the rest in the hiding place."

Silence. The child looks at Thanh. She says to him:

"I'm going to want you for the rest of my life."

She gives the big envelope with the money to Thanh, who knots it in a little scarf; he ties it around his waist, he tightens the knots in the scarf.

Then he says:

"Let him try to take it."

The child says:

"You shouldn't tell even me where you have hidden the money."

Thanh says he will never tell anyone, not even Paulo, who has no memory.

The child looks at Thanh falling asleep.

When they went to the sea wall in the B-12, Thanh sang to put the child to sleep—and, he said, to drive off her fear of demons, drive off her fear of the forest, as well as the tigers, pirates, and every other menace along the Asian borders of Cambodia.

Thanh falls asleep. The child strokes Thanh's body. She thinks about the forest of Siam and she cries.

So Thanh lets the child have her way, he sings for her again—she cries, she asks him why he doesn't want her. He laughs. He says inside him he has the fear of killing the men and women with white skins, that he has to beware.

This is again Cholon.

Sometimes the chauffeur arrives alone at the bachelor quarters. And sometimes the Chinese isn't there yet. He appears from who knows where, the Chinese, like a visitor, to visit the child.

169

The bachelor quarters are almost never locked, not even at night. The Chinese doesn't lock up. He says he knows the neighbors. Before her, they often had parties, the neighbors from the street and also neighbors from other streets. Later, he had gotten to know her and the parties came to an end. The child asked him if he missed those parties. He said he didn't know.

One evening, one of the last evenings, the black car isn't in the street by the high school. She is very frightened. She goes to Cholon in a rickshaw. He is there. Alone. He is asleep. He is in a very childlike position, curled up in his sleep. She, she knows he isn't sleeping. She looks at him for a long time without going over to him. He pretends to wake up. He smiles at her. He looks at her for a long time without saying a word. And then he holds out his arms and she comes and he lays her out against his body. And then he lets her go. He says he can't. That's when the idea of separation enters the room and settles like a stench you want to run away from.

He says his body no longer wants her, she who was leaving, leaving his body so alone and forever. Forever.

He didn't talk about the pain. He let her do as she pleased. He said that his body had started loving the pain, and that it was taking the place of the child's body.

This was something that remained unclear to her. He explained it badly.

You could say, yes, that he had loved her like a madman until it killed him. And that he now only cared for the sterile knowledge of that love, which was making him suffer.

170

But every evening the chauffeur waited for the child in the Léon Bollée.

He takes her in his arms. He asks if the gates to the boarding school don't close at a certain hour. She says yes, of course, but you can get in by the porter's gate. She says:

"He knows us. And if he doesn't hear us, we go behind the kitchens, we call a houseboy and he opens the door for us."

He smiles. He says:

"They all know you, the houseboys."

"Yes. We come and go as we please. We're like brothers and sisters. I speak Vietnamese with them, for them there's no difference."

The child is seized with rage, suddenly she looks barely in control of herself. She says:

"My mother knows that if I had to come in every night, I would take my little brother and Thanh and I would run away to Prey-Nop. To the sea wall."

The Chinese asks where it is exactly. She says it doesn't matter if he doesn't know. He repeats:

"To the sea wall. With Paulo and Thanh. She says it's like paradise."

She says yes, that's it, paradise.*

---

*Years after leaving, the child still dreamt of seeing Prey-Nop again, the path to Ream. By night. And the road from Kampot to the sea. And the dances at the canteen in the harbor at Ream, and dancing to "China Nights" and "Ramona" with the young foreigners who ran contraband along the coast.

He asks:

"Do you sometimes not go back to the boarding school at all?"

"No. But I told you—when my mother's here, I go to the Hotel Charner with her. I don't usually go to the movies by myself. My little brother often comes in with Thanh, we go together."

"Did you sometimes go to the sea wall alone with Thanh?"

"Sometimes a lot. For the planting, or to pay the workers after the rains."

She tells how they slept together on the same cot, how she was still too little for him to have her. How they pretended, pretended to suffer because they couldn't do it, pretended to cry because they wanted each other. She adds: Then he got into politics, and he fell in love with me.

The Chinese doesn't interrupt her anymore. He lets her talk. He watches her. She knows: it isn't her he sees, but the first rows of the Eden Cinema, where the half-caste girls go when they escape from the dorms at Lyautey.

She says:

"I don't usually go to the movies with Hélène, she gets bored, she doesn't understand a thing about movies. You have to understand, we don't pay at the Eden, we don't. Before, when my mother was in Saigon waiting to be assigned a post, she played piano at the Eden. So now the manager lets us in free—I forgot, I also go to the movies with my math teacher."

"Why him?"

"Because he asks me to. He's young. Saigon bores him."

"Do you like him?"

The child, doubtfully:

"So-so . . ."

"What about Thanh?"

She seems to be thinking it over. She says:

"How can I put it: I like him a thousand times better than my math teacher. I like him a lot, a whole lot. You know that."

"Yes."

"So why do you ask?"

"To suffer because of you."

Suddenly she is sweet. She says she likes talking about Thanh a lot.

He says he likes Thanh a lot too, that you can't not like him.

She also says that someday Thanh will go back to his village in the Elephant Mountains near Siam. He will be very near the lands by the sea wall.

They are by the channel for the Messageries Maritimes, where they've been going every evening during the big heat.

The chauffeur stops in front of a kind of stand covered with branches. They drink choum.

The Chinese looks at the child, he worships her, he tells her so:

"I worship you, I can't do anything about it," he smiles, "even by suffering."

The chauffeur drinks with them. In these places all three of them drink choum, they laugh together, but the chauffeur never speaks first to the child.

She looks at the Chinese, she wants to say something to him. He knows it:

"What is it?"

She says that this evening she wants to go back to the boarding school.

"For Hélène's sake," she says, "otherwise she'll wait up for me, and if I don't come, it will make her sad. And she won't sleep."

The Chinese looks at her:

"That isn't true."

"You're right, it isn't true at all."

She says:

"What is true is that I want to be alone for once. To think about you and me. About what has happened."

"And about nothing, too."

"Yes—and about nothing, too."

"Not about what will happen to you—no, I'm sure you don't ever think about that, about what will happen to you."

"I don't, you're right."

He says he knew it.

She smiles at her lover, she finds her way to him, she hides against his body. She says:

"I think life started for me with our affair. The first in my life."

The Chinese strokes the child's hair. He says:

"How do you know . . ."

"Because sometimes I want to die, to suffer, I want to be all alone—without you, so I can love you and suffer because of you and think about things I'm going to do."

She raises her eyes to him and she says:

"The way you also want to be alone."

"Yes." He adds: "Me, I leave you at night when you're asleep."

174

She laughs. She says:

"I leave you at night, too, but I thought you left me when you spoke Chinese."

She turns her face away. She tells him:

"Last month I thought I was going to have a baby. My period was almost a week late. At first I was scared, you get scared, you don't really know why, and then when I started bleeding, I was sorry . . ."

She falls silent. He takes her to him. She is trembling. She doesn't cry. She is cold from having said that.

"I had started thinking about what he would be like. I saw him. He was sort of Chinese like you. You were there with me, you were playing with his hands."

He doesn't say anything. She asks him if his father would have given in because of the child.

The Chinese is silent.

Then he answers. He says no, it would have caused a scene, but he never would have given in.

The child looks at him crying. She cries, too, hiding from him. She says they will see each other again, that it can't be any other way. He doesn't answer.

The child crosses the main courtyard at Lyautey Boarding School.

At the end of the hallway near the kitchens, the houseboys'

lamp is lit. The houseboy singing is the one from the paso doble. This evening he is singing a song that she knows by heart, the child, the one Thanh sang at dawn as they left the forest before Kampot.

The child liked crossing the main courtyard at Lyautey Boarding School, the covered playgrounds, the dormitories, she even liked being afraid in the middle of the night. And the young houseboys' longing for the white girls who came home late at night, she liked that the same way, too.

In the bed next to hers, Hélène Lagonelle is asleep.

The child doesn't wake her. And the child, as soon as she closes her eyes—she also falls into that shared, dizzying sleep of childhood.

The bachelor quarters.

They are side by side in bed. They don't look at each other. The Chinese is in terrible pain. The child feels her fear of Long-Hai come over her almost every evening now in the bachelor quarters. Her fear of dying over it.

Tonight it's Hélène Lagonelle she tells him about. She says she wants to bring her there. So he can have her. If she asks her, Hélène Lagonelle will come.

"I'd like that a lot, your taking her as if I had given her to you. I'd like that before we separate."

176

He doesn't understand. Her words seem to leave him indifferent. He doesn't look at her. She cries as she talks. He looks elsewhere—at the street, the night.

She says:

"It would be a little like she was your wife, like she was Chinese and she belonged to me and I was giving her to you. I like loving you when you suffer over me like this. I'm there with the two of you. I watch. I give you permission to be unfaithful to me. Hélène is seventeen. But she doesn't know anything. She is beautiful beyond belief. She is a virgin. She is enough to drive you mad, but she doesn't know it. Nothing, she doesn't know a thing."

The Chinese is silent. The child shouts:

"I want her for you, a lot, and I'm giving her to you. Don't you hear me?"

She has shouted it. The Chinese talks to himself. He doesn't talk about Hélène, only about his pain.

"I don't understand anything anymore, I don't know how this has happened, how I could let my father do this to me, let him murder his son the way he has."

Silence. The child lies down on her lover's body. She hits him. She shouts:

"She is very unhappy, Hélène. She is. She doesn't even know she's unhappy; all the boarders are in love with her, with Hélène. The counselors, the director, the teachers. Everybody. She couldn't care less. Maybe she doesn't see it, doesn't know it. But she can see you. You would take her the way you take me, using the same words. And then you would get us mixed up sometime, later, her and me. While you two are forgetting me, I'm watching you and crying. It's still ten days until we leave. I can't think about it, the picture of her and you is so clear . . ."

The Chinese shouts:

"I don't want Hélène Lagonelle. I don't want anything anymore."

She is silent. He falls asleep. He sleeps in the warm breeze from the fan. She says his name under her breath: this one time. She falls asleep. He hasn't heard her.

Suddenly, in the dark of night, the rain came. The child was sleeping.

As though from the depths of time and despair, the Chinese calmly said:

"The monsoon has started."

She had awakened. She heard.

The rain was pouring down on the city. It was a whole river covering Cholon.

The child went back to sleep.

Softly, the Chinese told the child to come see the monsoon rain, how beautiful and desirable it was, especially at night during the dog days that preceded it. She opened her eyes, she didn't want to see anything, she closes them again. She doesn't want to see anything. No, she says.

And she turned her face back to the wall.*

He is very pensive, very alone.

They are very alone. Already deprived of each other. Already distant.

Silence.

And then he asks the ritual question. They already talk just to talk. They tremble. Their hands tremble.

"What will you do in France?"

"I've got a scholarship, I'll go to school."

"What does she want for you, your mother?"

"Nothing. She wanted everything for her sons. So for me she doesn't want anything anymore. She may keep Paulo with her; I would have liked for him to stay with Thanh, there in the bungalow by the sea wall."

The Chinese asks about Thanh.

"Where does his family come from?"

"He doesn't know. He was too small when my mother took him away. It's funny, he doesn't remember his parents, doesn't remember anything but his little brothers and sisters. And the forest."

---

*She no longer knows where they were that first night of the monsoon rains. Maybe still at the café by the channel drinking choum, or in the large cat pavilion at the Jardin des Plantes listening to the black panthers crying for the jungle, or there in the bachelor quarters. She remembers the sound of the rain filling the arcade, crushing her body without touching it, the sudden relief of a body free from pain.

"He hasn't tried to find out about his brothers and sisters?"

"No. He says they couldn't possibly have survived."

Silence.

She climbs roughly on top of him. Stays there, against his body.

They cry.

She says, she asks:

"We'll never see each other again—ever?"

"Never."

"Unless . . ."

"No."

"We'll forget."

"No."

"We'll make love with other people."

"Yes."

Tears. They cry very softly.

"And then one day we'll fall in love with other people."

"That's right."

Silence. They cry.

"Then one day we'll talk about us with new people, we'll tell them how it was."

"And then some other day, later on, much later on, we'll write the story."

"I don't know."

They cry.

"And one day we'll die."

"Yes. Our love will be in the casket with our bodies."

"Yes. The books, they'll be outside the casket."

"Maybe. We can't know that yet."

The Chinese says:

180

"Yes, we know it. That there will be books, that we know."
It can't be any other way.

The sound of the rain again in the middle of the night.
Their bodies on the bed. They are still entwined, asleep this time.
We see them, they appear only dimly because of the black monsoon sky—the way we can tell who they are is from the child's short shape stretched alongside the long one of the North Chinese.

An alarm clock goes off in the darkened bachelor quarters.

The child gets up. Looks outside. The light still isn't the light of day. Remembers. And cries.
She showers. She hurries as she cries. She looks at the alarm clock. It is very early, not six o'clock yet. He must have remembered and told the chauffeur to set the alarm.

The sky is still dark, a night sky.

The chauffeur opens the door. He gives her a cup of coffee and a Chinese cake.
She remembers. She had forgotten her older brother was leaving.

The chauffeur is supposed to drive her to the docks of the Messageries Maritimes.

The chauffeur takes the route along the waterways. He drives fast.

We see them next in front of the Messageries' outer gate.

Thanh is there with the little brother, facing the big departures platform.

The sun rises in an indifferent gray sky.

About to sail, the ship is there alongside the pier: an ocean liner with three classes of service. That's the one.

There are the little brother and Thanh, "shut out" behind the high gate. The child joins them.

The mother is alone inside the gate with her older son. Pierre, the one who is leaving.

Otherwise there are only a few whites.

It looks like a prison transport.

Native policemen in khaki uniform and bare feet mix with the "shipboard passengers." There are always a few around the ocean liners when they sail. Because of the opium dealers, prison escapees, stowaways, a rabble of all races, all rackets.

In first and second class, the deck is occupied by Hindus who will disembark at Colombo and by other passengers of uncertain color who will probably disembark at Singapore.

This is an ordinary sailing.

The older brother is on the lower deck of the ship. He has come down from the first-class deck to be nearer the mother.

She acts as though she can't see him. He tries to laugh as if it were a joke. He doesn't see his sister and his brother. He looks at his mother, this woman who is ashamed, and bursts out sobbing.

He is leaving her for the first time. He is nineteen years old.

The child and the little brother cry on each other's shoulders, sealed in a despair they can't share with anyone else. Thanh has his arms around both of them, he strokes their faces, their hands. He cries over their tears, he cries over the mother's tears, too. For love of the child.

The mother. She is turned toward the ship. We can't see her face. She turns back. She comes over to the gate, leans against the gate next to the children who remain to her. She cries soundlessly, very softly, she is drained. She is already dead. Like Thanh, she strokes the two children's bodies, they who have been separated from the other, their older brother, a child ruined by his mother's love, a failure of God.

The ship's horn sounds.

The mother goes mad.

The mother starts running. She flees toward the ship.

Thanh opens the gate and catches up with her. He takes her in his arms. She doesn't resist. She says:

"I'm not crying because he is leaving. I'm crying because he is lost, I can see that, he is already dead. I don't want to see him again, there's no point anymore."

As the ship pulls away, Thanh keeps her from looking. The older brother goes off with his head down, he leaves the deck, he will not look at his mother again.

He vanishes inside the ship.

They had stayed there a long time, the three of them in one another's arms.

And then Thanh let go of the mother. She didn't look again. She already knows there is no point anymore. You can't make anything out anymore, neither bodies nor faces. Thanh is the only one still crying. He cries over the whole thing. Over himself, too, the orphan restored to his original status of abandoned child.

The door to the bachelor quarters is open. She goes in. The Chinese is smoking opium. He is indifferent to the child.

She comes over to him, lies down there against him, but just barely, almost without touching him.

She cries fitfully. He lets her. She is tender, as though distracted from him. He knows it.

Silence. He says:

"It's over."

"Yes."

"I heard the horn."

He also says:

"It's sad, that's all. There's no point crying. No one has died."

The child doesn't answer, seemingly indifferent from here on.

And then she says something she has learned from Thanh that very morning. That is, the mother has boarded her son with their former tutor, far away in Dordogne. She won't see him when she goes to France. That was another reason why she was so desperate at leaving him. She says:

"She feels guilt, a lot of it, for having neglected us over the years, Paulo and me. She thinks it's bad."

The Chinese talks about his marriage so the child will forget the older brother's departure. He says:

"She is coming to Sadec, my wife. This is the last visit before the wedding. I have to go to Sadec to pay her a call."

The child has heard. She is there all of a sudden, before him, ready to listen to this story which is stronger, more captivating than her own, the one from all the novels, the one about her victim, hers, the child's: *the other woman* in the story, still invisible, the one in every love affair.

The Chinese sees that the child has come back to him, she is listening. He goes on talking as he strokes her. He says, further: You know about it, it happens now the way it happened in China ten thousand years ago.

She asks him to tell her more.

"When I saw my wife for the first time, she was ten years old. I was twenty. The families matched us when she was six. I have never spoken to her. She is rich, like me. Our families matched us primarily for that, the equivalence of our fortunes. She is covered with gold"—he smiles—"with jade, with diamonds, like my mother."

The child listens the way he wants her to. She asks:

"And why else did they pick her?"

"Because of her family's high moral standards."

185

The child smiles, a little mockingly. The Chinese smiles too. He says:

"I sometimes forget how young you are, a child. It's when you listen to stories that I remember . . ."

She is still beside him on the cot. She hides her face against his chest. She is unhappy.

She doesn't cry. She doesn't cry anymore. The Chinese says, very low:

"My love, my little girl . . ."

The child touches the Chinese on the forehead:

"You feel as though you had a fever."

The Chinese looks at her at arm's length to see her better. He looks at her "forever all at once," before the love story ends.

He says:

"You want to tell me something . . ."

"Yes. I lied to you. I turned fifteen ten days ago."

"It doesn't matter."

He hesitates, and then he says it:

"My father knew it. He told me."

The child cries out:

"Your father really is disgusting, you know."

He smiles at the child. He adds:

"The Chinese like little girls, don't cry. I knew it."

She says:

"I'm not crying."

She is crying.

He says:

"I wanted to tell you something, too. I had them bring your brother some opium. He was as good as dead without opium.

186

He can smoke a little on the ship. I had them give him a little money just for himself."

She pulls away from him, mistrustful suddenly. She doesn't answer. He says:

"I would have liked to be able to make love to you. But I don't want you at all anymore. I'm dead to you."

Silence. She says:

"That's the way it should be."

"Yes. I'm not suffering at all. You do it, so I can watch you."

She does it. As she comes, she says his name in Chinese. She has done it. They look at each other, look at each other until the tears come. And for the first time in her life she says the standard words for saying it—the words in the books, the movies, life, for every lover.

"I love you."

The Chinese hides his face, stunned by the utter banality of the words the child has said. He says yes, it's true. He shuts his eyes. He says quietly:

"I think that must be what has happened to us."

Silence.

He calls her again.

"My little girl, my child . . ."

He kisses her mouth. Her face, her body. Her eyes.

A long silence fell.

He didn't look at her again. He took his arms away from her body.

He pulled away from her. He didn't move again. She gets scared like she did about Long-Hai.

She gets up, pulls on her dress, takes her shoes, her book-bag, and stands in the middle of the bachelor quarters.

He opens his eyes. Turns his face to the wall so as not to see her anymore, and says, with a tenderness she no longer recognizes:

"Don't come back."

She doesn't leave. She says:

"How are we going to manage . . ."

"I don't know. Don't ever come again."

She asks, she says:

"Ever again. Even if you call me."

He hadn't answered. Then he did. He said:

"Even if I call you. Ever again."

She leaves. She closes the door.

She waits.

He doesn't call her.

It was when she reached the car that he cried out.

It was a dark, long cry, of impotence, anger, and disgust, like something vomited. It was a cry voiced from ancient China.

And then suddenly the cry thinned out, it became the discreet complaint of a lover, a woman. It was at the end, when it was nothing more than sweetness and oblivion, that the strangeness had come back into that cry, terrible, obscene, immodest, unreadable, like madness, death, passion.

The child hadn't recognized any of it anymore. Not a word. Nor the voice. It was a death call—whose, which, which animal's, you couldn't really tell, a dog's maybe, yes, but also a man's. The two merged in the pain of love.

A bus on a road: we recognize the one from the ferry.

The child is on that bus.

She is going to Sadec. She is going to see her mother.

The door is open. We think there's no one there. The mother is there, in the living room, she is asleep, stretched out in her rocking chair. She is in the draft from the door. Her hair is uncombed. Near her, crouching against the wall, there is Thanh. The child goes in. The mother wakes up. She sees her daughter. Her smile is very sweet, a bit ironic. She says:

"I knew you would come. What were you afraid of?"

"Of your dying."

"It's the other way around. I'm relaxing. It's like a vacation. I'm not scared they'll kill each other anymore. I'm happy."

Her voice breaks. She is crying. Silence. She starts looking at her daughter. She laughs through her tears as though she were discovering her.

"Where did you get that hat?"

The girl smiles at her mother through her tears.

The mother smiles too, thinks about it, she doesn't see her daughter's tears, she sees the hat.

"I have to say—it suits you. It's different. Did I buy you that?"

"Who else?" she smiles. "There are days when we can make you buy anything we want."

"Where was this?"

"Rue Catinat, it was a final mark-down."

The mother looks like she's been drinking. She changes the subject abruptly. She asks:

189

"What will Paulo do . . ."

The child doesn't answer, the mother persists:

"There must be things he can do, now that he won't be afraid anymore."

The child says he will be afraid for the rest of his life.

The mother puts the question to Thanh:

"What do you think Paulo might do later on?"

Thanh answers the child:

"He could be an accountant. He is good with numbers. He could also be a mechanic. He is very good with cars. But it's true, he'll be afraid for the rest of his life."

The mother doesn't want to talk about the fear. She says:

"Yes, that's often . . . that's true: children like him, who are behind, they're often very good with numbers, geniuses sometimes"—tears again—"I haven't loved Paulo enough, maybe it's all because of that . . ."

Thanh says:

"No. You shouldn't think that way. It's in the blood, in the family."

"You think so?"

"I'm sure of it."

Silence. The mother says to her daughter:

"You know, I've given up. The Land Registry has finally agreed to buy back the upper lands, together with the bungalow. I'll pay off our debts with that money."

Thanh looks at the girl and signals no, that what the mother is saying isn't true. The mother doesn't see Thanh. If she did, she wouldn't care.

Silence. The child looks at the bare walls. She says:

"They took the furniture."

190

"Yes. The silver, too. I'm saving the 500 piastres that are left for France."

The child smiles. She cries out:

"We're not giving them to the Chinese or the chettys anymore. We're not paying anymore."

Now the mother smiles and cries out:

"Yes. That's all over now. All over." Suddenly she is talking like her children. "Let them ask—not a cent."

The three of them laugh.

Paulo has heard them laughing and comes in. He sits down beside Thanh, leans against the wall like him. And he laughs, too, at the mother's immense, still unequaled laugh. "A north country laugh," the older brother would say.

The child says:

"No need to worry about me, either, someone's bound to marry me someday."

The mother strokes the child's head. Paulo smiles at his sister.

Then Thanh and Paulo go out. They are going to get the cold, unsweetened tea the mother drinks every day on Thanh's advice to "cool her blood."

The mother and the daughter remain alone.

The mother "dreams" about this child, her own, who is there beside her.

"It's true—they like you, men. You must know that. And also that if they like you, it's for what you are. And not for your money, because you haven't got any money, never have . . ."

They stop laughing.

And then there is silence. And the mother questions the child.

"Are you still seeing him?"

"Yes." She adds: "He told me never to come back, but I go just the same. We can't help it."

"So you aren't seeing him just for the money."

"No." The child hesitates. "Not just."

Surprised, sorrowing now, the mother says in a low voice: "You've become attached to him?"

"I guess so."

"A Chinese . . . how strange . . ."

"Yes."

"So you're unhappy."

"A little."

"How awful. My God, how awful . . ."

Silence. The mother asks.

"You came with him?"

"No. I took the bus."

Silence. Then the mother says:

"I would have enjoyed seeing him again, you know, that man . . ."

"He wouldn't have wanted it."

"It wouldn't have been for the money, but for him. The money"—she laughs—"I've never made so much of it."

They laugh. They have the same youthful laugh.

The child looks at the places where the rosewood furniture has been taken away by the usurers.

She asks if the doors on the piece in the living room didn't in fact have hazelnut trees and squirrels carved on them. She says: I've already forgotten.

The mother looks at the marks the piece has left on the wall. She doesn't remember what it was like, either. She says:

"If you ask me, it was water lilies, it's always the same here, water lilies and dragons. It is so nice to be going back with nothing, no furniture, nothing."

The child asks:

"We're leaving when, exactly?"

"In six days at the latest, unless there is some unforeseen delay"—silence—"by the way, I sold my beds to the chettys. For a lot. They were in very good condition. I'll miss the colonial beds. The beds are too soft in France. I sleep badly in France, but so what."

Silence.

The mother says:

"I'm not taking anything. What a relief—my bags are packed. I just have to go through my papers, your father's letters, your papers from French class. And then there are the coupons for Samaritaine, for winter clothes—I can't forget them. You don't realize how soon fall will come once we're in France."

The mother has fallen asleep. The child goes out, pokes around, observes, recognizes things.

Thanh is in the kitchen, he is washing the rice for that evening. Paulo is with him.

It seems like an ordinary day, a day from before all the changes that have taken place since the last vacation—eight months ago.

The child pokes around the house. Furniture is missing. They've taken the old sewing machine from Dô's room.

The beds are still in the bedrooms, they've got tags on them with writing in Chinese.

The child goes into the bathroom. She looks at herself. They haven't taken down the oval mirror.

The image of the little brother crossing the courtyard passes through the mirror. The child calls to him very softly: Paulo.

Paulo came into the bathroom through the small door facing the river. They kissed a lot. And then she took off her clothes, and then she lay down beside him and she showed him how he should come onto her body. He did what she told him. She kissed him some more and she helped him.

When he cried out, she turned toward his face, she covered his mouth with her own so that her mother wouldn't hear her son's cry of release.

That had been the only time in their lives they made love together.

It was the kind of orgasm the little brother hadn't known until then. Tears ran from his closed eyes. And they had cried together, without a word, as they always had.

It was that afternoon, in that sudden confusion of happiness, in her brother's sweet and mocking smile, that the child realized she had lived out one love between the Chinese from Sadec and her little brother in eternity.

The little brother had fallen asleep on the cool tiles of the bathroom floor.

The child left him there.

She went back to her mother in the living room.

Thanh is there again.

The mother is drinking the iced, bitter tea. She smiles at Thanh, she says she will never drink tea like his in France.

She asks where Paulo is. Thanh says he doesn't really know, he has probably gone to the new municipal swimming pool. The child and Thanh haven't looked at each other since she's come back into the living room.

The mother asks the child whether she is still going to school. The child says no. Except for French, for the fun of it.

"What are you expecting?"

"I'm not expecting anything."

The mother muses. She says:

"Yes, that's the way to put it—we're not expecting anything anymore."

The child strokes her mother's face, she smiles at her.

It's at this point the mother tells her child what makes them different, has always made them different.

"I've never told you, but you should know—I didn't have your gift for schoolwork. And anyway, I was too serious, I was that way for too long; that's how I lost my taste for pleasure . . ."

The mother also tells her child:

"Stay the way you are. Don't ever listen to me again. Promise me. Not ever."

The child cries. The child promises:

"I promise."

To change the subject, the mother suddenly, disingenuously, brings up the Chinese:

"They say he's getting married."

No answer from the child. The mother says softly:

"Answer me. You never answer me."

"I guess that's right. That he's getting married. Here in Sadec, in the next few days actually. Unless he spits on all of it at the last minute: his engagement, his father's orders . . ."

The mother is stunned. She cries out:

"Do you think he could do that?"

"No."

The mother is despondent but calm. She says:

"Then there's really no hope."

"None at all."

The mother, rambling, alone, but still calm:

"No, you're right. Chinese children are brought up to respect their parents. They're like gods to them, it's almost disgusting. But maybe I could talk to him one last time, one last, last time, do you think? I could explain to him—what would it cost me?—I'll explain our situation very clearly. At least let him not desert you."

"He'll never desert me. Never."

The mother closes her eyes as though she were about to go to sleep.

Her eyes closed. She says:

"How can you know that?"

"I know it the way people know that someday they'll die."

196

The mother cries softly. She says through her tears:*

"What a mess. My God, what a mess. And you—will you forget him?"

The child answers, against her will:

"Me—I don't know; and if I did, I certainly wouldn't tell you about it."

The mother's eyes are youthful, alive. Freed from having to have no hope, she says:

"Then don't say a thing."

The mother asks her daughter:

"So there are things you don't tell me, or not?"

The child lowers her eyes. She braces herself, says there are, but it doesn't matter. The mother says that's true. That it really doesn't matter.

Paulo has come back. The mother asks him where he has been. Paulo says: at the municipal swimming pool. It's the little brother's first lie.

The child and Thanh smile. The mother doesn't know a thing. The little brother sits down beside Thanh.

Thanh casually "reveals" the mother's behavior toward her older son. The mother listens to that as she would anything else, she seems to find it interesting, appropriate. Thanh points at her. He says:

"She gave him another 500 piastres. She had to. She said that otherwise he was going to kill her, kill his mother. And it was true, she knows it."

---

*The author would like to stick with these "disjointed" conversations, which have a *found* spontaneity. You might call them *"layered," parallel conversations.*

The child looks at her mother, who is unmoved. Openly dissembling.

The child asks Thanh what he did about it:
"So what did you do?"
The mother listens with interest. Thanh answers:
"I wrote his father that your older brother had stolen the money that was left. Then his father writes back telling me to come see him. I went. He gave me another 500 piastres for her. She took them. That makes up for it. And Pierre, he's gone, he can't rob her anymore."

The mother looks as though she were asleep, worn out by her own self, by all the stories that involve her—her own included—without her precisely knowing how, in what way.

Paulo laughs maliciously, the way he might laugh at a practical joke. He says, he asks:
"His father, he's paid for everything."

The child looks at the mother. She goes to kiss her. The mother bursts into silent laughter. Little cries emerge from her body. And then they all laugh, a family in hysterics. They are happy because the little brother has spoken without having been urged to do so.

The child asks if the father has paid for everything—just like that—without conditions.

Thanh laughs. He says the only condition the father laid down was that they clear out of the colony.

They all laugh until they are in tears, especially Paulo. Thanh goes on:
"His father wrote to our mother to tell her her son had run up debts in every den in Sadec, and even in Vinh-Long. And

198

since he is a minor, eighteen years old, the mother is responsible for her son's debts. If the Chinese father doesn't pay up, our mother will lose her job, and then she won't have any income, and then in the end she goes to jail."

The mother has listened attentively. And now, suddenly, she starts laughing again, screams with laughter. She is frightening. She says:

"And what if I don't want to go back to France anymore?"

No one answers the mother. As though she hadn't said a thing.

And in fact she no longer does say anything.

The child says to Thanh, in "Thanh talk":

"The father paid all our debts on condition that we clear out, is that right?"

"That's right."

The little brother laughs. He repeats it too, slowly:

"On condition that we clear out."

Thanh laughs like a child. He says:

"That's right. Also, the 500 piastres that Pierre stole—the father has paid them back for Pierre, because otherwise Pierre can't smoke, and not being able to is awful. He is in bed all day. He may kill himself. So the father, he gives him the 500 piastres." (Pause.) "After that the father, he wrote a second letter to the mother, in French, telling her she has to clear out, that he has had enough of this business with the brother, the opium, and on and on with the brother, and the money on and on—and all the rest."

A burst of laughter from all present, from the mother and Thanh as well as the little brother and the child.

"And in the letter," Thanh continues, "there was another 500 piastres for her. In his letter, the father, he says not to say anything about it to the mother. Because his son doesn't know about it. He doesn't want his son to know about the money he is giving the mother."

Smiling, the child asks Thanh:

"How do you know all of this?"

"Because. People, they talk to me. And I remember, I remember for all of you, even Pierre, even the Chinese father. Sometimes he tells me the story of his family when they get out of China, me, I fall asleep, he keeps going."

And they all laugh with Thanh.

And then the mother stopped listening. Everyone starts talking in lowered voices. The past bores the mother.

And then the child goes into the courtyard. She leans against the garden wall. And Thanh comes to join her. They breathe one another in and he kisses the child on the mouth for the first time and he says that Paulo is his love, too. She says she knows. She says his name:

"Thanh."

She says he will go to Siam and other places, too, to Europe, France, Paris. For me, she says.

"Yes. For you. Yes, when you're all gone, I go back to Prey-Nop, and then Siam."

"Yes. I know. Have you told Paulo, too?"

"No. I've said only to the Chinese and you. No one else."

"Why the Chinese?"

The child gets scared. She asks Thanh if he isn't going to try and find his parents, if he isn't talking nonsense. Thanh says he hasn't thought about it once since they discussed it, she and he, except about his little brothers and sisters, but you can't find little children in the forest of Siam again. Ever.

The child comes back to her question:

"Why did you talk to the Chinese about it?"

"So I can see him again after you're gone. To be friends with him. So we can talk about you, Paulo, our mother"—he smiles—"so we can cry together over loving you."

The B-12 is on the road. It's Thanh driving. The child is beside him. He is driving her back to Saigon. They are supposed to stop by the bachelor quarters before going to Lyautey. The child is frightened. She tells Thanh that. Thanh says he is frightened for the Chinese, too.

In Cholon.

The Léon Bollée is there with the chauffeur. The chauffeur comes over to the child, he smiles at her. He says the master has gone to play mah-jongg, he will be back. The chauffeur tells the child the bachelor quarters are open. That it was the master who requested it in case she arrived before he did.

Thanh had gone back to Sadec.

The child goes into the bachelor quarters. She looks around. Maybe so she won't forget. Then she gets undressed, showers, climbs into bed in his spot, along the wall, there where she finds the Chinese scent of tea and honey. She kisses the place where his body would be. She falls asleep.

When the Chinese comes in, dawn is breaking.

He gets undressed. He lies down alongside her. He looks at her. Then he says softly:

"You're so little in my bed."

She doesn't answer.

Her eyes closed, she asks:

"Did you see her?"

He says yes.

She says:

"She's beautiful."

"I can't tell yet. But I think so, yes. She is tall, full-figured, much more so than you." (Pause.) "She must know about you and me."

"How would she know?"

"Through the little maids of Sadec, maybe, that's what you told me: they're very young, they're your age, fifteen, sixteen years old, they're curious. They know all about everything that happens in all the houses on all the posts."

"And you, how would you be able to tell . . ."

"By nothing. By everything. I don't know."

The child says it's the beginning of a marriage to wonder about things like that.

The Chinese hesitates and he says:

"Maybe, yes. I haven't talked with her."

"Is it always like that in China?"

"Always. For centuries now."

She says:

"We don't understand that at all, we others. You know that . . ."

"Yes. But we understand. So we can't understand you when you say, at the same time, that you don't understand."

The Chinese is silent and then goes on:

"We know absolutely nothing about each other, and that, too, is something to talk about, and understand—and the things you don't say, the way you look at one another."

"She has gone back to Manchuria."

"No. She has left Manchuria forever. She is living with my aunt in Sadec. Her parents are arriving tomorrow to prepare the chamber for the newlyweds, the nuptial chamber you call it."

"Yes."

The child has gone to stretch out in the armchair. The Chinese is smoking opium. He seems indifferent.

She says they no longer hear the American record or the waltz the young man used to play on the piano. The Chinese says he may have left the street.

Then the Chinese tells the child to come over next to him.

She goes over as he wishes, up against his body. She puts her mouth to his mouth. They stay like that. She says:

"You've smoked a lot."

"That's all I do now. I have no more desire. I have no more love. It's wonderful, incredible."

"As if we had never met."

"Yes. As if you had died a thousand years ago."

Silence.

She asks:

"What day is the wedding?"

"You'll have left for France. My father, he got the information at the Messageries Maritimes. All three of you are on the departures list for the week before the wedding."

"He pushed the wedding date back."

"I wouldn't have cooperated if you were still here."

The child asks if he knows through his father about all the money the older brother has stolen, about all of the complications with the mother.

He says he doesn't know, but it doesn't interest him. It's nothing for his father, nothing at all—petty theft, not even worth discussing.

She says they may see each other again at some point. Later on. Years from now. Just one time or many times. He asks—why see each other again?

She says:

"To find out."

"What?"

"Everything that will have happened in our lives, yours and mine . . ."

Silence.

And then she asks him, over and over, where he saw his fiancée for the first time. He says:

"In my father's living room. And also in the street when she came to my father's house to show herself to me in his presence."

"You told me she was beautiful."

"Yes, beautiful. Beautiful to look at, I think. Her skin is white and very delicate like the skin of the women from the north. She is whiter than you. But she has a full figure, and you're so small and slender . . . I'm afraid I may not be strong enough."

"You can't pick her up . . ."

"I don't know, maybe. But you—you weigh as much as a suitcase. I can throw you on the bed like a little suitcase."

The child says the phrase "full figure" will always make her laugh from now on.

"She still isn't allowed to look at me. But she has seen me, you can be sure. She, she takes the Chinese customs very seriously. Chinese women, they assume a wife's role once they have been allowed to see us, near the end of the engagement."

He looks at her with all his strength. He bares her face with his hands to see her to the point of unmeaning, of not recognizing her anymore. She says:

"I would have liked us to get married. To be married lovers."

"So we could make each other suffer."

"Yes. Make each other suffer as much as possible."

"Until it killed us maybe."

"Yes. Until it maybe killed your wife, too. Like us."

"Maybe."

"By the suffering I'm causing you, her and you, you will also be married through me."

"We already are married by you."

She is crying very quietly, very softly, she says she can't keep from crying, she can't . . .

They stop talking. There is a long silence. They don't look at each other again. And she, she says:

"And then there will be the children."

They cry. He says:

"You will never know those children. You will know all the children on the face of the earth, but those, never."

"Never."

She leans against him. With a slight gesture, he makes a place for her against his chest. She cries against his skin. He says:

"It's you I will have loved all my life."

She sits up.

She cries out.

She says he is going to be happy, that she wants him to be, that she knows it, that he will love this Chinese woman. She says: I swear it.

And then she says there will be those children and that children are happiness, every one, that they are the real spring-time of life, children.

As though he hadn't heard her, he looks at her, looks at her. And he says:

"You are the love of me."

He cries over the springtime of children that she, she will never see.

They cry.

She says she will never forget his scent. He says that for him, it will be her child's body, that nightly rape of her skinny body. Still sacred, he says. He will never know that happiness again—desperate, crazy, death is easier, he says.

The long silence at night's end has finally come. And a driving rain crashes down on the city again, drowning the streets, the heart.

He says:

"The monsoon."

She asks if such heavy rains are good for the rice paddies.

He says they're the best.

She raises her eyes to this man. Through her tears she looks at him again. She says:

"And you will have been my love."

"Yes. The only one. In your whole life."

Rain.

Its scent reaches into the room.

A very strong desire, beyond recall, makes the lovers take each other again.

They fall asleep.

Wake up.

Fall asleep again.

The Chinese says:

"The rain, here, with you, one time more . . . my little girl, my little child . . ."

She says it's true, since they met this was the first time it had rained. And twice in one night.

She asks him if he has rice paddies. No, the Chinese never do, he says. She asks what business they do, the Chinese. He says: gold, a lot of opium, also tea, a lot, and porcelain, too, lacquerware, local blue wares, "Chinese export blues." He says there are also the cubicles and the stock market. It's everywhere

207

in the whole world, the Chinese stock exchange. Also every-where in the whole world now, people are eating Chinese food, even swallows' nests and hundred-year-old eggs.

She says:

"And jade, too."

"Yes. And silk."

And then they stop talking.

And then they look at each other.

And then she pulls him to her.

He asks: What is it?

"I'm looking at you."

She looks at him for a long time. And then she tells him that sometime he must talk to his wife about everything that happened—between you and me, she says—between her husband and the girl from the school at Sadec. He will have to talk about everything, the happiness as well as the suffering, the despair as well as the joy. In order for people—anyone who wanted to, she says—to tell it over and over again, for them not to forget the whole of the story, for something very precise to remain, you'd have to give the names of the people, the streets even, the names of the schools, the movie houses, even the houseboys' songs at night at Lyautey and even Hélène Lagonelle's name, and Thanh's, the orphan from the forest of Siam.

The Chinese had asked: Why his wife? Why tell her rather than others?

She said: because for her it's the pain that will make her understand the story.

208

He asked again:
"And if there is no pain."
"Then it will all be forgotten."

He was in the back of the big black car that is parked along the wall of a warehouse in the port. In his usual dress. The raw tussore silk suit. As though he were sleeping.

They don't look at each other.

See each other.

The same crowd as always on the docks when an ocean liner sails.

An order is shouted over the tugboats' loudspeakers.

The propellers begin turning. They chew, churn the river water.

The noise is awful.

It is frightening. It is always frightening at this point.

210

Everything. That one might never see this thankless land again. That one might forget this monsoon sky.

He must have shifted on the back seat, over to the left. To gain a few seconds and see her one more time for the rest of his life.

She doesn't look at him. Nothing.

And now, here comes that popular tune, that "Desperation Waltz" from the street. There is always farewell music, nostalgic and slow, to ease the pain of separation.

Even those who are alone then, who haven't come to see anyone off, share in the strange tragedy of "going away," of "leaving" forever, of betraying the destiny they realize was theirs just as they lose it; and they, too, have betrayed it, all on their own.

Toward the first-class passenger decks, that's where he must be looking. But she isn't there, she is further down the same deck, she is with Paulo, who is already happy, already on his way into the voyage. Free, my little brother, my loved one, my treasure, come out of terror for the first time in his life.

The unmoving racket of the engines swells, becomes deafening.

She still doesn't look at him. Nothing.

When she opens her eyes to see him again, he is no longer there. He is nowhere. He has gone.

She closes her eyes.

211

She won't have seen him going by again.

In the darkness behind her closed eyes she finds the scent of silk, tan silk, skin, tea, opium.

The idea of the scent. Of the room. Of his captive eyelids, beating beneath her kisses, the child's.

The cries, the names, the tragedy of an ocean sailing recur along the docks.

He must have vanished very quickly after the ocean liner cleared the end of the dock. While she was looking for her little brother on deck.

They pull up the gangplank.

They weigh anchor with a din like the world ending. The ship is ready, on its own. It floats on the river.

You think no, it can't be.

And it is done. The ship has left land.

You shout.

The ship is floating on the waters of the river basin.

It still needs a hand, needs setting straight in the channel, on the clean axis of the river and the sea.

A delight, the ship very slowly responds to orders. It sets itself straight on a certain unreadable and secret course, the one to the sea.

The sky, already resounding with the ship's horn, filled with black smoke—just for fun, it seemed, but no.

And then, for the rest of the child's life at that hour of the day, the sun had reversed its course.

She remembers.

In front of her, her elbows on the railing, there was that brown-haired girl, also looking at the sea and, like her, crying over everything, over nothing.

She remembers that she had forgotten it.

From the stern of the ship, a young man had come along, dressed in a dark jacket, like in France. He was wearing a camera on a strap across his shoulder. He was photographing the decks. He leaned out over the railing and photographed the liner's bow as well. Then it was the sea itself he photographed. Then nothing more. He was looking at the tall brown-haired girl, who had stopped crying. She had stretched out on a deck chair and was looking at him, they were smiling at each other. The tall girl waited. She closed her eyes, she pretended she was sleeping. The young man didn't come over to her. He went on with his walk along the deck. So the tall girl got up from the deck chair and went over to him, the young man. They talked. Then they both looked at the sea. And then they started walking together along the promenade deck for first-class passengers.

The child didn't see them again.

She is stretched out on a deck chair. You might think she was asleep. No. She is watching.

On the planking, on the ship's bulwarks, on the sea, with the course of the sun through the sky and the ship, an unreadable and wrenching script takes shape, takes shape and destroys itself at the same slow pace—shadows, spines, shafts of broken light refocused in the angles, the triangles of a fleeting geometry that yields to the shadow of the ocean waves. And then, unceasingly, lives again.

The child wakes as they reach the high seas, as the ship is about to take a westerly course toward the Gulf of Siam.

In clear weather, you can see the ship very slowly losing height and at the same time very slowly sinking into the curve of the earth.

The child had fallen asleep on the deck chair. She didn't awake until they were on the open sea. She cried.

Beside her, there were the two passengers who had come back and were looking at the sea. And who, like her, were crying.

It is still quite hot. They haven't reached the cold wind yet, the salt, stinging wind of the high seas. They will reach it after the first waves, after rounding the farthest point of the delta, beyond the last of the rice paddies on the Plain of Reeds and then the point at Camau, the farthest reach of the Asian continent. Of the word, *Asia*.

The decks are no longer lit. They are still filled with people waking or still sleeping on deck chairs. Except the first-class lounge, where people are always up, day and night, and far into the night, usually until morning, playing cards and dice and talking loud, laughing or angry, and all of them drinking whiskey sodas and Martel Perriers and Pernod, too, no matter what the nature of their voyage, business or pleasure, and no matter what the voyagers' nationality, what the game.

The first-class bar was the safe haven on this voyage. The summit of childish oblivion.

The child looks in at the bar, of course she doesn't go inside, she heads over to the other deck. There's no one there. The passengers are on the port side, waiting for the wind from the open sea. On this side of the ship, there is only a very young man. He is alone. He is leaning on the railing. She walks past behind him. He doesn't turn toward her. He probably hasn't seen her. It's strange he should be unaware of her to such an extent.

She couldn't see his face, either, but she remembers his unseeing face as being like the journey not taking her in.

Yes, that must be right, he was wearing a kind of sport coat. Blue. With white stripes. He was wearing pants the same shade of blue, but solid.

The child went over to the railing. Because the two of them were so alone, on this side of the ship on that deserted deck, she would so much have liked for them to talk. But no. She waited a few minutes. He didn't turn around. He wanted to keep to himself, that's what he wanted more than anything in the world, to be by himself. The child moved on.

The child had never forgotten that stranger, probably be-

215

cause she would have told him the story of her love affair with a Cholon Chinese.

When she turned around at the end of the deck, he was no longer there.

She goes below deck. She is still looking for the double cabin where they have their berths, she and the mother.

And then, all of a sudden, she stops looking. She knows there's no point, there won't be any finding the mother.

She goes back up to the promenade deck.

The child doesn't find her mother on that deck, either.

And then she sees her, she is further off this time, she is still sleeping, in another deck chair, slightly turned toward the bow. The child doesn't wake her. She goes back below deck. She waits some more. Then she takes off again. She is looking for her little brother, Paulo. And then she stops looking for him. And then she sets off again below deck. And she lies down there, in front of the double cabin for which the mother has forgotten to give her the spare key, and she remembers. And she cries.

Falls asleep.

A loudspeaker announces that they are out of sight of land. That they have reached the open sea. The child hesitates and then goes back on deck. A very slight swell has set in with the ocean breeze.

On board ship, night has fallen. Everything is lit up, the decks, the lounges, the gangways. But not the sea, the sea is in darkness. The sky is blue in the black night, but the blue of the sky isn't reflected in the sea, no matter how calm it is or how black.

The passengers lean on the railings once more. They are looking toward what they no longer see. They don't want to miss the first waves arriving off the high seas, and with them, the cool of the wind suddenly falling across the sea.

The child is looking for her mother again. This time she finds her sleeping the sleep of an immigrant in search of asylum. She lets her sleep.

Night finally fell. In a matter of minutes it was there.
A loudspeaker announces that they will begin serving in the dining room in ten minutes.

The sky is so blue, the wind is so cool, people hesitate a little, but finally, regretfully, move toward the dining room.

The mother is there, at a table. Early as always. She is waiting for her children. She must have gone to her cabin, she's just back. She has changed her clothes. She has put on the dress Dô made for her, a dark-red silk with little pleats, but the pleats are too big and make the dress droop every which way. She has combed her hair, the mother, she has put a little powder on her face and a little color on her lips. In order not to be seen, the mother has picked a corner table for three.

The mother had always been in awe of traveling by ocean liner. She realized she had never made up for the education she missed as a young peasant from the north country, the person she had been, until she sailed the seas to see what life was like in other places.

The child had never forgotten that first evening on the ship.

The mother complained in a low voice and said that if Paulo didn't come to dinner he was going to throw off the service completely. Then the mother asked the waiter not to serve them just yet. The waiter said service stopped at nine o'clock, but he would wait a little longer. The mother thanked him as though he were saving her life.

They had waited over a quarter of an hour in silence.

The dining room filled up. And at one point when the door opened behind the mother, it was in fact Paulo, the little brother. He came in with the tall girl who had been with the photographer when the ship sailed. Paulo saw his sister without looking at her. The mother pretended she was interested in all those people in the dining room and in them only.

Paulo gives his sister a pleading look. She understands she isn't supposed to notice him. The young woman looks at her, too, she recognizes the little girl from the deck who was so alone and crying, she smiles at her. The mother is still looking out into the dining room, which is full. She is her usual self, not quite in control, bewildered, comic, the usual.

The child looked at the mother while Paulo went by, and she smiled at her.

They don't talk while their dinner is being served.

It was at this point in the evening, with the abruptness of disaster, that the horror had surfaced. People shrieked. Not words, but howls of horror, sobs, shouts that broke off in tears. It was something so dreadful that no one could express it, say it.

It was growing. People were shouting everywhere. It came from the decks, the engine room, too, the sea, the night, the whole ship, from all around. At first isolated, the shouts became a cluster, a single outcry, rough, deafening, frightening.

People run, want to know.

And then they cry.

And then the ship slows down. With all of its strength the ship slows even further.

People call out for silence.

Silence spreads throughout the ship. Then there is silence.

It is in this silence that we hear the first words, the shouts come back, almost low, muted. Of terror. Of horror.

No one dares ask what has happened.

In the silence, you can hear clearly:

"The ship has stopped. Listen. You can't hear the engines anymore . . ."

And then the silence returns. The captain appears. He speaks into a microphone. He says:

"There has just been a terrible accident in the bar—a boy has jumped overboard."

A couple comes into the dining room. He in white, she in a black evening dress. She is crying. She says to everyone:

"Someone jumped overboard. He ran past the bar and threw himself over the railing. He was seventeen."

They go back on deck. The dining room has emptied out.

All the passengers are on deck. The shouting gives way to very low crying. The horror of it has penetrated everything, deeper, more terrible than the shouting.

The mother and the child cry, they've stopped eating.

Everyone has left the dining room. People wander aimlessly. Women cry.

Some young people, too. All the children have been brought up from the cabins. The women keep them close by, hugging them to their bodies.

In the dining room, only a few people remain, the same ones the world over: the ones who are hungry *just the same,* who want their dinner, who rudely summon the waiters, who say *they have a right to their dinner, to be waited on, that they've paid for it.* They are the ones no one responds to anymore these days.

The waiters have left the dining room.

In the distance, a man's voice says the lifeboats are being lowered, to back off from the railings.

People still want to see.*

"Seventeen, the son of the administrator at Bien-Hoa. There's a woman friend of the family in second class who talked with the captain. They didn't find anything in the child's cabin—no note for his parents, nothing; he was going home to France. A brilliant student. A wonderful boy . . ."

Silence. Then the murmuring begins again:

"They'll never find him . . ."

"He's too far off now . . ."

"It takes an ocean liner several miles to stop . . ."

The child hides her face, she says quietly to the mother:

---

*The voices blend together, like in the empty salons of *India Song.*

"We're lucky Paulo came in before. We would have been afraid . . . how awful . . ."

The mother hides her face too, she crosses herself, she says softly:

"We should thank God and ask forgiveness for even thinking that."

Again, the surge of voices:

"We'll move on at dawn. That's the worst of it, that moment . . . giving up hope . . ."

"Ships have to wait twelve hours before starting up again . . . or for sunrise. I don't remember which anymore . . ."

"The empty sea at morning, it's so awful . . ."

"Abominable, a child who refuses to live. There's nothing worse."

"Nothing, that's the truth."

An almost complete silence reigns on board the stopped ship.

People still put their faith in the lifeboats. They watch the searchlights sweeping the surface of the sea.

There is still hope, it hasn't been totally abandoned, the word is murmured, but they do say it:

"You have to keep hoping. You have to. The sea is warm in these latitudes. And he, he can swim for a long time, he is so young . . ."

"You think it will stay warm all night . . ."

"Yes. And it isn't a strong breeze, that counts for something . . ."

"And God is there, let's not forget . . ."

"That's true . . ."

More tears. They stop.

"The worst of it would be if he saw us and no longer wanted anything."

"Neither life nor death . . ."

"Yes, that's it."

"He should wait a bit more and try to figure out what would bring him back toward the outline of the ship."

Suddenly, with the same abruptness as the accident, music filled the decks, the lounges, the sea. It came from the music room. "Someone who doesn't know," is what people say.

Someone says he had already heard the piano before the accident, but far off, as though from another ship.

A voice shouts it's someone who doesn't know, who hasn't heard the shouting. He ought to be told . . .

The music is everywhere, it fills the cabins, the engine room, the lounges. Very loud.

"Someone should go warn him."

A clearer voice, young, says no:

"Why tell him?"

Another voice. This one is crying:

"Absolutely not, ask him instead not to stop playing for anything, not for anything; he has to be told it's for a young boy—especially that kind of music, he must know it, you hear it everywhere . . ."

The street music that's in vogue with young people just

then, that talks about the wild happiness of first love and the unrelieved, incurable pain of having lost it.

The word spreads that the music coming from the room should be allowed to continue.

The whole ship listens and cries over the young stranger.

The child has left her mother. She is looking for the music room.

The whole ship is in darkness.

The music room is at the very front of the ship. It is lit by the reflection of the searchlights on the sea. The door is open. The child suddenly feels something like hope in her heart. What if everyone was wrong. What if it were true that you never know, you never really know, never, everyone says so.

She goes to the door. She takes a look.

This one has black hair. He is wearing a white, custom-tailored suit. He must be older.

She waits a little longer. Looks again. No.

It isn't that. It will never be that again, that wanting to die in the few seconds before moving toward the railing.

That's over.

The child stretched out on the floor under a table against the wall. The piano player didn't hear or see her. He was playing that popular and desperate waltz from the street without a score, from memory in the darkened room.

The light entering the room is still from the reflection of the searchlights.

The music had penetrated the stilled ocean liner, the sea, the child—not only the living child playing the piano, but the one who was floating with closed eyes, unmoving, suspended in the heavy waters of the deep.

Years after the war, hunger, death, camps, marriages, separations, divorces, books, politics, communism—he had phoned. It's me. She recognized him as soon as she heard the voice. It's me. I just wanted to hear your voice. She said: Hello. Everything frightened him, like before. His voice trembled, and that's when she recognized the North China accent.

He said something she hadn't known, about the little brother—that his body had never been recovered, that he had never been buried. She didn't answer. He asked if she was still there, she said yes, that she was waiting for him to speak. He said he had left Sadec because of his sons' schooling, but that he would go back there eventually because it was the only place he wanted to go back to.

It was she who asked about Thanh, what had become of him. He said he had never heard any news of Thanh. She asked:

Nothing ever? He said: Never. She asked what he thought it meant. He said that in his opinion Thanh had wanted to find his family in the forest of Siam and that he must have gotten lost and died there, in that forest.

He said that to him it was strange how much their story had remained what it was before, how he still loved her, how he would never stop loving her for the rest of his life. How he would love her until he died.

He heard her crying on the telephone.

And then from further off, probably from her room—she hadn't hung up—he could still hear her crying. And then he tried to hear still more. She was no longer there. She had become invisible, unreachable. And he had cried. Very hard. With all the strength that was in him.

The images suggested below could be used to punctuate a film based on this book. These images—called insert shots—would under no circumstances "explain" the story, or draw it out or illustrate it. They would be scattered through the film as the director chooses, and would in no way determine the story. The images proposed here could be reshot at any time, by night, by day, in the dry season, in the rainy season. And so on.

I see these images as an exterior to the film, a "country," the one the people in this book are from, the world of the film. And of the film alone, with no attempt to reproduce reality.

Examples of images for these insert shots:

A blue sky bursting with light.

An empty river in all its immensity in an uncertain, relative night.

Daybreak over the river. Over the rice fields. Over the straight white roads crossing the silken expanse of the fields.

Another river in all its breadth, its vastness. Only the green line of its banks is unmoving. Between its banks it advances toward the sea. Complete. IMMENSE.

The roads of French Cochin China in 1930:

The roads' straight white reaches, with a procession of children driving their oxcarts.

A river seen from higher up. Crossing the expanse of the Plain of Camau. Mud.

Daybreak dimming the light from the sky.

A day of a different blue, dying.

Between the sky and the river, an ocean liner. It skirts the banks of the green immensity of rice.

The ocean liner beneath the straight monsoon rain, lost in the flooded expanses of rice.

The straight monsoon rain and nothing more, that straight rain across the entire frame. Straight, like no place else.

The dark river very close up. Its surface. Its skin. In the nakedness of a clear night (relative night).

Rain. On the rice paddies. On the river. On the huts in the villages. On the thousand-year-old forests. On the mountain chains bordering Siam. On the upturned faces of the children who drink it.

The Gulfs of Annam, Tonkin, Siam, seen from above.

The rain ending and disappearing from the sky. The clarity that replaces it, pure like a naked sky.

Naked sky.

Children and the yellow dogs who keep watch, who sleep in the full sun before empty huts.

The millionaires' American cars slowing down in these villages because of the children.

Children, stopped, looking on without understanding.

The boat villages. By night.

By day. At morning. In the rain.

Peasants walking barefoot and single file on the embankments. For thousands of years now.

The children and the yellow dogs playing. Their mingling. The charm and grace of their togetherness.

And the troubling grace of the ten-year-old girls who beg for coins in the village markets.

And voiceovers would come in, too: